ON A FORSAKEN LAND FOUND

ANTHONY W. EICHENLAUB

Print ISBN - 978-1-950542-12-3

Ebook ISBN - 978-1-950542-11-6

oakleafbooks.com

Cover Art by: Anthony W. Eichenlaub

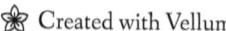 Created with Vellum

To all those who have woken from a very long sleep to find everything changed.

CHAPTER ONE

Amongst the golden grass, under a sapphire sky, Ash Morgan lay for a silent moment to contemplate the vast and many consequences of scientific success. Often, success meant increased responsibilities, and she was no exception. She owned a share of the responsibility for every experiment performed in the expanding biolab. Scientists throughout the colony of Edge depended upon her input.

Other times, success meant the broadening of scientific opportunities—fields of studies previously undreamed of. Her success had certainly offered that. Her colleagues in the biolab not only created plants and animals, they designed robust ecologies to fulfill multiple-layered functions of a robust ecosystem.

Still other times, success meant being mobbed by dozens of adorably feral guinea pigs, cuddling with little piles of fluff as they emerged from the grass, and hoping they wouldn't soil the lacy pink dress, which read, *STUPID* across the back, because even an undeniably successful scientist sometimes lost the occasional, completely unfair wager.

Nearby, the toddler Skye played in the red-brown soil. Mud caked his hands and smeared his face.

"I don't understand," said Hector. The big guy lay next to her, mauled by his own herd of guinea pigs. "What were you going to make Simon wear if you won?"

"The same dress," Ash said.

"But it would have looked good on him."

"That's not the point!" Simon had beaten her at a game of chess. "It was a fluke."

"Seven flukes, I heard." She could hear the smile in his voice.

"I called for a rematch." Ash turned to look her boyfriend in the eyes. "Several times."

Hector shrugged his massive shoulders. "It sounds to me like you're bored."

"Moira cut off my access to the Archives!" It meant she could no longer delve into Earth's historical record. No music. No videos. No books. "For no good reason."

"I heard there was fire involved."

"Seems to me you hear a lot of things."

The fluffiest guinea pig wriggled up onto her chest and nuzzled her chin. She gave it a little scratch behind the ears and said, "*You* wouldn't take my queen too early in the game, would you, Mr. Floofers?"

"You know there's not a rule against that, right?" Hector said.

"It's called sportsmanship," Ash said. "Plus, I was trying to perfect my queen's gambit."

"Do you even know what that means?"

"It's when the queen does something awesome." She booped Mr. Floofers on the nose. "Probably."

"Lookit me, Auntie Ash!" called Skye from halfway up the wall of her house. His little nubby claws dug into the fiber-formed building. It was only a six-foot drop, but Ash was almost positive that was too much for a toddler.

A regular toddler anyway. "How did you get up there?" Ash asked. "Did you climb my house?"

"I just went up." His voice had a peculiar accent, like his tongue didn't move quite right. Several months of speech therapy ended with the conclusion that Skye's voice was different because *he* was different. Thanks a lot, registered and qualified speech development experts.

Skye *was* different. As the first of the first wave of modified humans called skylings, Skye bore fleshy ridges along his nose, nubby claws at the ends of his fingers, and razor-sharp teeth. Along with the teeth, apparently, came a reworked jaw and oddly shaped tongue. It made him growl whenever he talked, which was absolutely precious. Ash wasn't sure what this did to help the kid survive, but he was better adapted for the rocky planet of Sky than Ash would ever be.

Ash, after all, needed to wear a rebreather to filter particulates from the air while Skye breathed without any assistive technology. She folded her hands behind her head and closed her eyes, basking in the warm blue sun.

"Should we get him down?" Hector asked as Skye scrambled higher.

"Kids need to learn their own limits." Ash picked at a piece of grass. "My parents let me fail and look how great I turned out."

Hector let out a puff of air, but Ash couldn't tell if it was a laugh. "My grandparents hovered over me constantly."

"Grandparents always retired early in my borough." Ash didn't like the dark place that line of thinking led, since *retirement* was a euphemism for being murdered by the AI Traverse and recycled for biomass, so she added, "I guess having grandparents around is what made you so good at what you do."

"Construction?"

"Helping people," Ash said. "Doing things that actually matter to real, live human beings."

She ran her fingers through the fine grasses growing around them. The blossom storms had changed over the last year, and there were fewer and fewer all the time. The soil built up in the crevices and cracks of the broken landscape, creating an adequate growing medium for what few plants they had introduced to the environment. Finding appropriate seeds in the databanks wasn't hard, but choosing the appropriate varieties for their climate was. When they finally found a species of *miscanthus* that tolerated the soil and engineered a variety of microbes that could help it fix nutrients, they'd planted it everywhere. Its feathery floral spikes waved gently in a cool wind and provided both food and home for an ever-growing population of guinea pigs.

Success meant a scientist could relax, breathe deep, and simply enjoy life.

Ash took one of Hector's big arms in both of hers. She moved in close to him, and he didn't seem to mind. "How's it going doing things that matter anyway?"

"Biology matters," he said.

"You build houses that people *live* in. I build an ecology where everyone eventually dies."

"Well, you're just going to need to cure death."

Her back straightened.

"No, Ash. You can't cure death."

"But what if—"

"No."

"If the telomeres—"

"No."

She held tight to Mr. Floofers and scooched even closer to Hector, letting her whole self press gently against him. Quietly, under her breath so that he couldn't possibly hear, she muttered, "Essential oils..."

"I heard that," said Hector, mirth leaking into his voice. "And that's not real science."

"Flavor crystals?"

"It's just crystals. Flavor crystals are something Earth people made lemonade out of. I'm pretty sure the only crystal involved is sugar."

"Sugar crystals don't count as science."

"Don't let Juliette hear you say that food science isn't important." He shifted his weight and put an arm around her. They'd spent their lunch hours like this every day for the last several months, and he always made her feel at ease. "But I doubt nutritional supplements are going to help us live forever."

She stared up at the sky. "There are a lot of things we haven't tried with pickle juice."

"What's bothering you, Ash?" How the hell did he know? "You always do this when something's bothering you."

"Do what?"

"Deflect."

"I'm afraid the guinea pig population is out of control."

"Stop it."

Mr. Floofers made eye contact with Ash, and wet warmth spread across her chest.

She shot a pleading look at Hector.

"Did you train him to do that?"

"Maybe." She hadn't. Mr. Floofers was a born genius.

"I'll print you a new dress." The big man rose from the grassy ground, scattering guinea pigs to the earth. He took a couple steps and ducked his head through the door of Ash's little house.

Ash closed her eyes and basked in the warm sun. All around, guinea pigs scurried through the tall grass, and a gentle breeze brought with it the scent of life on the barren planet of Skye. She must have dozed, because when she woke the breeze had stopped and all she smelled was the heavy scent of urine.

Ugh, guinea pig pee was the worst. She opened her eyes.

That was the moment Skye chose to fall off the roof.

Hector caught him in one hand as he emerged with a shoulderless black dress and a fuzzy pink shawl.

"Your comm unit keeps beeping," he said.

"Oh, crap!" Ash grabbed the dress from Hector and ran for the biolab. "Take Skye back home for me," she called back. "Thanks!"

By the time Ash walked into the meeting room wearing the new dress, she was already annoyingly late.

The scientists Gerald and Leonard sat at one end of the table, Cynthia dominated the other. Olympia sat at the head nursing two babies. A third baby lay quietly in a custom-designed spider walker baby carrier next to her seat. On her other side sat a stand with a blank screen thrust up at an angle—an opportunity for Victor to grace them with his presence.

"How nice of you to join us," said Leonard. He had his explosion of gray hair braided, and it made his head look small. "We were just wrapping up."

Gerald fixed his twitchy gaze on Ash, but said nothing.

"I want to talk about the atmosphere," Ash panted.

Leonard let out the biggest sigh Ash had ever heard.

"Again?" Cynthia asked. Her large body pressed forward against the table. "You bring this up once a month."

"It's important!"

"Particulate concentration hasn't gone down," Ash said. "Oxygen levels—"

"Doesn't that just tell us your crapstorms failed?" said Leonard, bushy eyebrow raised. The logical implications being that therefore nobody should listen to her.

When Ash gestured at the wall screen, a map of their surrounding area appeared. "The weather has stabilized, and the soil is established, but oxygen levels are rising, even after all those blossom storms."

She gave the scientists a moment for a collective eye-roll, which they used to its fullest, those jerks. Nobody ever called them blossom storms, even though they were a result of Ash's fantastic and completely successful biological experiment.

"So it's a failure?" Olympia said.

"I'd call it a mitigated success," Ash said.

Cynthia scoffed. "So, you're saying your calculations were wrong?"

Ash brought the first overlay onto the map. It showed particulate density, wind, conditions, and oxygen levels. "My latest survey shows that when the wind changes, the particulate levels change."

"What does that mean?" Olympia asked, appearing genuinely curious. She rotated one baby out and pulled the third in. All three bore the same modifications of Skye but kept their mother's gorgeous brown skin and thick hair.

The screen next to Olympia flickered to life, showing Victor's angular and darkly handsome face for a second, then fading to gray. Victor was having technical problems again, then. He'd be no help.

Ash zoomed her map way out and showed more of the unknown terrain. Miles and miles of it, but at the edges, the terrain blurred. Photos from the space station wouldn't focus on anything so far from the colony. The AI allowed her to process local conditions in deep detail but wouldn't allow her any details on land more than a hundred miles from Edge.

"If we don't do something, we'll always have to wear rebreathers," Ash said. "The particulates will never go away."

"Is that so bad?" Leonard asked. "I think I look pretty good with my face covered."

"No you don't, Leonard," Ash said. Before he could respond, she said, "There's more. Oxygen levels are actually still increasing. At this rate, it'll be fifty years before it's toxic to us, and another hundred before it's toxic even to Skye, but it'll get there. This will be a dead planet again, no matter what Traverse does."

"So, your crapstorm project failed," Leonard said.

The room was silent for a long time. Acid burned in Ash's belly. "I haven't failed," she said through her teeth. "None of this would have been apparent before my blossom storms." Ash met the gaze of every person in the room, making sure each understood the importance of what she was saying. "Any ideas what we can do?"

After several painful seconds, Leonard said, "You're asking?"

"Yes?" Ash drew the word out into a question.

Olympia said, "It's just that you don't usually ask others for help."

"That's because I usually have all the answers."

"I mean," Leonard said, "we usually *end up* helping, but it comes in the form of cleaning up your messes."

"Like the time you gave Simon boils," Olympia added.

"It wasn't contagious!"

The other scientists looked at Ash with expressions that were far too judgey.

"It wasn't *very* contagious in the simulations. Plus, once we got it under control, we really learned a lot."

"The flies," Gerald dared, glaring at her with dark eyes.

"I was printing a worm that would help aerate the new soil."

"Those were maggots."

Ash mumbled, "They aerated the soil." Before emerging by the millions and blotting out the sky for a few days. "And that problem solved itself." They all died.

Gerald's jaw tensed, but he said nothing else.

Olympia sighed. "Does anyone have suggestions that might help with the problem Ash brings to the committee?"

After a long pause, Leonard said, "We've refined our nectar fermentation process with the help of visitors from Anvil."

Ash shot him a dry look.

He gave her a weak smile. "It sounds like we're going to need a drink to celebrate all of these mitigated successes."

"Think on it, everyone," Olympia said. With that, she closed the meeting.

One by one the other scientists filtered out the room. Ash collapsed into one of the chairs and placed a cold hand on her forehead. They hadn't listened. She'd failed.

Again.

Success as a scientist meant a reintroduction to failure because a good scientist was defined by her failures, not her successes.

As Olympia bustled her babies out of the room, she touched Ash on the shoulder. "They'll work on it," she said.

Ash wasn't convinced. She touched her friend's warm hand. "Thanks for trying, though."

"Simon told me you'd be wearing a special dress to today's meeting."

"I was," Ash said. "I had to change. Tell Simon there was a guinea pig mishap."

"There always is, isn't there?" The door swung shut, leaving Ash alone in the meeting room.

Sometimes the consequence of success was that everyone still thought the scientist was a failure and nobody would take her seriously ever again. Ash's microbes had helped fix the planet's atmosphere. That it wasn't enough could hardly be considered her fault.

As she was about to leave, Victor's image appeared on his screen. His camera focused on her, and he smiled a wide, toothy grin. "Miss Morgan."

"Hey, Victor."

"I know the source," he said through his smooth accent.

"Excuse me?"

"I heard what you said, though I could not see. I know where the source of your problems lies, and there is somewhere that you can find information that will solve this problem."

Ash stood across from Victor's image. She didn't trust the man, but he knew more of the vast world of Sky than he had ever shared with the colony. "What's there?"

"Far from here you will find a desert, and in that desert, you will find answers."

"What's the catch?"

"Before you go, you must promise to do everything exactly as I say. A deviation from the rules I give you will mean disaster for you and your colony."

Ash leaned forward in her seat and looked straight into Victor's camera. "I'm listening."

Sometimes scientific success brought with it the confidence to dare an expedition into the great beyond, to venture where others feared to tread. Sometimes success and ragged persistence gave a scientist the clout to—over the protests of the most respected leaders of the community—assemble a multi-colony, multi-disciplinary collaboration to rival the most ambitious aspirations ever seen on the planet of Sky.

And sometimes success placed the scientist and everyone she had ever met in serious, mortal peril.

Such are the consequences of success.

CHAPTER TWO

Hector set his giant spider walker down on a flat expanse of shale at the edge of a vast stretch of gray-black sand. Blue sunlight burned through the cockpit window, and the horizon danced with watery mirage. A short distance away, an ebony pylon jutted from the sand, towering above the dunes. Its two truncated pyramids flanked an arch towering over the sand below.

"This is it," he declared, as if he weren't pronouncing their absolute doom. "The start of the road to Pyramid. From here, we walk."

"We can probably ride a little farther," Ash said, eyeing the harsh terrain. It had taken months to gather the group, supply the voyage, and arrange for everything they needed for a successful expedition. She knew this point was coming, and it still set butterflies loose in her belly.

They were about to walk farther than any of them had ever walked before, through the depths of a hostile desert under the guidance of unknown stars. No matter how she spun it, this was dangerous.

Hector said, "Victor's instructions were pretty clear. Don't bring any tech past this first pylon, never enter the pyramid at the center of town, and don't wander outside during the day if Traverse is in the sky above."

"He was probably joking," Ash said.

"Victor is the least humorous person I've ever met."

"That's why this isn't very funny. He also told me to bring you."

Hector furrowed his brow. "Is he able to imagine a world in which you left me behind? Who would carry all your stuff?"

"See? Not very funny."

She sealed her rebreather and wrapped a thin red scarf around it. The effect worked, she thought, in combination with her expertly tied turban and the layered black robes she'd crafted before they left. A pair of wide goggles completed the protective layer against the desert environment.

A gust sent shining silver-black sand across the open ground for miles upon miles. This far inland from the great ocean, the land became a dry, scoured wasteland where the stones had long since been pulverized by a million years of relentless wind.

Ash hopped out of the spider and slapped it on the side to alert those inside. Her legs were stiff from hours in the seat. The jet-black exterior of Hector's spider bore patches of crimson where it had been repaired after a fight against a kraken—a fight that it had won.

Three days' journey by spider had brought them this far. Two days' walk would get them to the lost colony. Victor's colony. Pyramid.

The source. Ash bent down and felt the fine sand between her fingers. This desert was the source of sediment in the air. Wind here carried fine dust high into the atmosphere. It spread across the entire world. How could she ever stop that?

"All right," she said, trying to keep the exhaustion from her voice. "Everybody out."

The spider's abdomen compartment opened to reveal Juliette's round, smiling face. Ash watched as the plump woman crawled from the back of the spider, her skin pink from the effort. She had blonde hair and her smile revealed infuriatingly deep dimples.

"You have to help me," Juliette whispered as she brushed past Ash.

"What?"

Seth's heavy boots sent up clouds of dust when he dropped down. Wiry muscles stretched under deeply tanned skin. Seth wore a sleeveless tunic and loose black pants. His goggles were thin, narrow things that protected his eyes but preserved his bemused expression and exquisitely chiseled cheekbones. Seth originated in Edge but had spent the past several months in Victor's reform program tending crops and operating heavy machinery.

"I'm just sayin'," Seth said to Juliette, "it's every man for himself out there. We'll have a better chance of getting what we need."

Juliette rolled her eyes.

Ash folded her arms. "Is there a problem?"

Seth followed Juliette. "In and out. Fast as possible. It's the only way."

Juliette waved him off.

"We're here to study the place," Ash said. "Not smash and grab. This is a scientific operation, aimed at discovery and information."

"You hired us and said you'd pay in first salvage rights," said Seth.

Ash said, "This is primarily a science outing, and you agreed to come because we wanted someone from each of the three settlements."

Behind Seth came the brother and sister Harish and Palak, new arrivals from the Anvil colony. Harish was a big man, with dark skin and a mole on the corner of his mouth that twitched when he was amused, which was basically never. Palak's skin was also dark, but the irises of her eyes were ringed with a fiery yellow. She was shorter than Ash and had mercilessly copied her exquisitely practical fashion down to the mirrored goggles and a poorly wrapped turban to cover her deep brown hair.

"I've loaded food and water into everyone's packs," said Juliette, "in case we become separated." She gave Ash a look that could not be deciphered. "Except for Ash's, which, by request, has been left completely empty to leave space for 'treasure and loot.'"

"Treasure and loot?" Seth accused.

"It's a figure of speech," Ash murmured. "Slang for discovery and information."

"I'm carrying her food," Hector said.

"Figures," said Seth.

"What's that supposed to mean?" Ash said.

Seth shot a questioning look at Hector, who shrugged. The big man's pack was the largest of the lot, but he was taller even than Harish, and despite his belly, he probably carried more muscle than the whole group combined. Hector could manage a little extra, and he always seemed happiest when he could help make Ash's life a little easier.

As far as Ash could tell.

They walked by night, guided by the billion stars decorating the dome of the sky and the road leading north into the desert. At times, the obsidian gates of the pylons that marked their desert journey towered high into the night sky. Other times, only a smooth dome of stone peeked over the top of a dune.

Each of Sky's seven moons made an appearance

throughout the night, from far-off Seven to the looming, blue One.

"These are the stupidest moon names ever." Ash said, hours into their first day of walking.

"I like it," said Seth. "Keeps it simple."

Ash shot him a glare. "Back in Earth's solar system, they named the moons of Jupiter after gods and goddesses."

"Yeah," said Seth as she walked up ahead, "but they still called it 'The Solar System.'"

Ash spun on him, fists on her hips. "They didn't know there were others when they first named it."

Seth peered up at the stars. "Pretty hard to figure that one out."

Hector passed the two, his heavy feet making tracks in the black sand. "People on Earth weren't very smart." Lot of help he was.

"Why did I even bring you?" Ash asked.

Hector shifted the weight of their supplies on his back, as if it had become uncomfortable. "For the rich tenor of my singing voice?"

Ash didn't even know he could sing, so she pushed forward so that she could drop the conversation.

As she passed Palak, the younger woman said, "I agree with you."

"That people on Earth were smart?"

Palak shot her a sideways grin. "No. That the names of our moons are stupid, except for the fourth one."

The fourth moon was named Marta. Ash had fought for that naming because it had been the full moon the night Marta changed their world forever by almost bringing Traverse's full wrath down upon them. It had also been the night she died.

"Maybe the others are just waiting for their names," Palak said. "Patiently."

"Moons aren't patient," Ash said.

Harish, who walked a few paces ahead of his sister, said, "Moons are the most patient things in the night sky. They go around and around, waiting for something that they do not ever understand."

"Bah." Ash couldn't get any help. She dropped back to speak with Juliette. "We should camp soon."

Juliette looked at the sky and consulted a chart. "We can walk for another hour."

"Do you ever feel like people don't value the work you do?" Ash asked.

"I make food."

Ash assumed that meant *yes*.

Three pylons later, a breeze picked up, and Ash pulled her robe close to brace against the driving sand. "Is it supposed to get this windy?"

Hector had their tent set up before the worst of the wind hit. They huddled inside, out of the driving howl. Ash curled against Hector and slept.

After what seemed like seconds, he moved, provoking her protest. He stretched, dressed, and left the tent, abandoning her.

Then, he made to disassemble the tent.

"I'm still sleeping," Ash mumbled.

The tent collapsed around her.

"Hey!"

By the time she extracted herself, the rest of the group had their packs ready to go. "You could have given me a warning."

"Gave you about a dozen warnings," Seth said.

Palak nodded.

"If we hurry," Seth said, "We can spend tomorrow night in the safety of the colony."

Ash thought that sounded like something the leader should say, but her head was too sleep-deprived to protest. "Exactly. So, let's go."

Ash wasn't convinced it would be safe, but she accepted a protein bar from Hector and started walking while he rolled up their tent. Her legs protested from the previous day's journey, and every step caused little sparks of pain to run up her calves. Every step on the fine, black sand felt like walking through mud.

"I'm just saying they should name them after gods," said Ash as the moon called One crested the horizon.

Palak said, "Most of the people I've met down here are atheists. Many aren't even superstitious."

"Gerald believes in some kind of generic life force."

Palak stared up at blue One. "Is that the guy who keeps making guinea pigs?"

"Victor believes that Traverse is a god," Ash said.

"Which moon do you think should be named Traverse?" Palak asked, mischievous smile sparkling in her eyes. "After our planet's vengeful god?"

Naming something in the sky Traverse seemed like an invitation for confusion. "Maybe we should just name them after Earth gods."

"But this isn't Earth."

"It's earthlike."

Palak gave her a skeptical look.

"Numbers aren't very sexy," said Ash.

"I didn't know sexy was the goal," Palak purred.

Seth, from behind them, said, "Sexy is always the goal, ladies."

Palak rolled her eyes.

Hector called from atop the next rolling dune, "I think I see something."

A pylon of pure silver shone in the moonlight from the sand a short distance away. Its surface glinted in the light of both One and Marta.

"Victor warned us about this one," Ash said, stepping close to the pylon. "If it's active, it's really dangerous, but he didn't think it would be."

"Should we go around it?" Seth asked.

Ash shook her head. "It's the entry through a protective barrier. Everywhere else is worse."

"How do we know if it's active?" Hector asked.

Ash had absolutely no idea. "It'll hum and there's a bunch of lights."

"So it's fine," Harish said.

"Probably."

Harish stepped forward, but Ash held him back. "Wait."

He said nothing, his eyebrows raised.

"I'd feel really bad if I'm wrong about it being inert," Ash said.

"You're going to test it?" Hector said.

"That's the plan." That wasn't really the plan. She looked to each of her traveling companions. "We're all sure we didn't bring any tech?"

Seth patted his pockets and gestured that he had nothing. Everyone else did the same.

"All right." Ash drew a long breath, then stepped through the pylon arch.

Nothing. A gentle breeze dusted her with grit.

Hector's jaw dropped in horror. "That was your test?"

"It's not active," Ash said.

The others passed one by one, each breathing a sigh of relief as nothing happened.

"We're close," Ash said.

Seth's grin showed a row of crooked teeth. "Then it's treasure and loot."

Ash bristled. "We are looking for a solution to our planet's atmospheric problems. It took us three months to put together this mission and every one of you promised that the entire focus would be on scientific discovery regarding damage being done to our atmosphere."

Juliette singsonged, "Or anything regarding agriculture or food production."

"Weapons tech," said Palak. When Ash shot her a dirty look, she shrugged and said, "It could be useful."

Seth barked a sharp laugh. "Like I said. Treasure and loot."

"We should have brought our own weapons, really," Palak said.

Ash tried to keep the annoyance from her voice. "I told you, we don't need Marta's energy weapon."

"But even a spear would be better than nothing."

"Victor wasn't sure if the residents would still be alive," Ash said. "But we're not going to attack them if they are. No weapons."

"You think they'll be friendly to visitors?"

"Maybe." Probably not.

"What if they're not?"

"Then I'm going to fill this backpack with tech and run away really fast."

That got a toothy grin from Seth. "I like how you think." He stepped up his pace and pulled ahead of the group.

"You're going to have to reign him in," said Juliette when he was out of earshot.

They crested the next dune, black sand shifting under their feet. Far ahead, in the light of the moon, sat a shimmering mirage of a dark city in a haze of shattered glass. The black smudge on the horizon stayed a thousand miles away with every step.

Then, when Ash's legs felt like they might fall off and the winds of morning picked up, they stepped through the dust of a particularly fine-sanded dune that butted up against the black gates of a city behind which towered a black pyramid of metal and glass that blotted out the night's already dark horizon.

"We're here," she shouted. "Welcome to Pyramid."

CHAPTER THREE

To Ash's great surprise, the expedition did not go horribly awry the second they stepped through the black gate. They sheltered in the black-walled alcove, hiding from the furious winds until the sun set and the wind died.

At dusk, Ash squeezed through a narrow gap in the open gate. The walls inside the long entryway were organic, like black bands of corded muscle tensed against the storm outside. Fine sand covered every surface, filling the notches in the walls with the gray-black dust and choking the corners of the enclosed space. Above, the arch of black metal blotted out the sky.

"It's like Victor's kraken," Hector said touching the segmented arc of a section of wall. "Like tentacles all coiled up."

Juliette's eyes were wide. "It's creepy."

Ash's every step echoed in the empty silence.

Across a long room, an arched doorway stood open to reveal the pyramid in the center of the city. It loomed in the dust-filled distance, a monolith watching over the city. Halfway up its sides, embedded in the decorative ridges, were enormous plates of black steel. Between the pyramid and the gate stood rows upon rows of dull, black structures, some squat like the fallen bones of a dead giant and some stretching upward like fingers clawing at the gray sky.

"Well, let's get out there, then." Seth crossed to the far gate.

Juliette shot Ash a look. Leadership. Right.

Ash cleared her throat. "Juliette, Seth, set up camp here. The rest of us will establish the perimeter."

Seth spat. He walked back to the center of the room and dumped his pack on the floor.

Juliette set her pack down and said, "Make sure to get back by sunrise."

Ash fixed Seth with her best glare, but he was already busy setting up a food printer. "Everyone moves in pairs. Harish and Palak, you map out the nearby area along the outer perimeter. Hector and I will see what we can find a little farther in. Any sign of trouble, come back here. No looting."

Seth latched a printer component in place with all the attitude of a disgruntled teenager. Ash watched him for a moment, sure he would protest more.

Finally, with a nod to Palak, she took Hector by

the arm and led him through the inner arch into the dead city.

The settlement was a long-dead leviathan. Black sand piled against abandoned buildings. Stone and dull iron formed the brutal architecture of the colony, with the drooping menace of the almost-organic tentacles emerging from the corners of dark buildings. Ash's heart pounded every time they rounded a corner. In places, arches over the street inert tentacles dangled like curtains. She took Hector's hand in hers and kept him close, just in case he was scared too.

He probably was, but the expedition didn't go horribly awry.

They mapped the streets with paper and pencil, making notes for places that required more attention later. The day stretched on, and the only sounds from the city were the wind blowing across the open ribs of a long road leading from their gate to the central pyramid.

"What was it like living here?" Ash asked from atop a black spire. She sketched the city's layout from above, saving them the tedium of wandering every street. Sections of town below gaped open like festering wounds, while others appeared to be clean and new. In the center of it all stood the pyramid. It must have always been in their thoughts the way it loomed above them.

"They really liked tentacles," Hector said. Everywhere they looked, the tentacles emerged in clusters from walls.

"I bet they were really into interpretive dance."

"You're going to need to back that up with archaeological evidence."

———

THE MORNING WAS HERALDED by a sound so loud it shook Ash's bones. It rang like a hammer on an anvil in a single strike that raddled her teeth. The rest of the night had been spent making maps. Between her map and the one Palak and Harish produced, they now had a good idea of half the moonlit city.

"What is that anyway?" Seth asked.

"It comes from the pyramid," Ash said. They wouldn't venture into the pyramid, so the deeply unnerving sound made no difference to them.

At least, that's what she told herself.

That day, Palak argued with Seth about the relative merits of the spears and knives.

"A knife is quick," Seth said through a mouthful of protein that Ash *knew* tasted like bland socks. "Easier to carry around and you can sneak up on someone with it and stab it in their neck."

"Spears have reach. They'll win the fair fight every time."

Seth scoffed. "If we're fighting fair, the fella with the gun's always going to win."

Ash listened as they went back and forth for hours on the subject until Hector whispered in her ear, "They're probably flirting."

"Oh." Ash nestled up next to Hector and listened instead to the howl of wind outside the entryway gate. The storm raged until she fell into a deep sleep.

———

ON THE SECOND NIGHT, Ash made pencil reproductions of some odd language she found in a nearby library. She couldn't interpret the language, but with enough samples she might eventually be able to decipher their meaning. From the diagrams on some of the charts, she thought it might contain designs for some important tech—or possibly the instructions for a game. More study was required.

Meanwhile, the rest of the team made more maps of the surrounding area, tracing the conduits that ran below the city streets through the various basements of buildings. It was tedious work, but every hour they spent in the city brought more answers.

And even more questions.

"Why do they have a wall?" asked Palak as the wind howled that day. "What were they keeping out?"

"Maybe there were monsters," Seth suggested, sitting next to her.

Palak bristled. "This is serious."

"Whatever." Seth tossed the remains of his food on the ground and sulked off to sleep against the wall.

"I don't think they're flirting anymore," Ash whispered.

Juliette said, "He hasn't figured that out yet."

Ash couldn't sleep. Her chest hurt with displaced worry. Her expedition hadn't been a catastrophic failure. Not yet. So why was she so worried?

———

HECTOR TENTATIVELY POKED one of the tentacle clusters just outside their entryway door. "What if the tentacles wake up and decide to tear us to shreds?"

"I find that highly unlikely." Ash absolutely did not.

"We should get in close to the pyramid here," Seth said, pointing at the joined maps. "That looks like a cluster."

"We're not going anywhere near the pyramid," Ash said. When Seth's wiry muscles tensed, she said, "It's dangerous."

"These here are junctions," Seth said, pointing to several points on the map. "Victor taught me how they work. They'll be the next best place to look for tech, outside the pyramid itself."

"Fine," Ash said. She considered how Seth and Juliette didn't get along. "Harish, you go with Seth and check this one here. Palak and Juliette, scope around this one. Hector and I will head down the long street and go there."

"By the pyramid," Seth deadpanned.

Ash traced a shape on the map. "Do you recognize that?"

Hector narrowed his eyes. "Nope."

"This is like Edge."

Nothing in this colony was like Edge. Not the tech, not the architecture, not the feel. Yet, in the shadow of the pyramid lay a Commons building like a warped parody of the one in Edge. Its domed roof loomed over the same oddly shaped town square.

"I need to see what they have instead of a biolab." She hoped it actually *was* a biolab but did her best to tamp down any expectations.

Ash led Hector through town to the square in front of the Commons building, taking the time to inspect buildings as they went. They weren't as different from Edge as Ash had originally believed. Some of the residential buildings even matched the three-room layout of her own house. By the time they found the square, the sun hung heavy against the horizon. Where the biolab's west wing was in Edge, sat a crater of twisted metal parted like the scorched ruins of a super-hot explosion. Inside the remaining half of the building, where her lab had stations, this had cluttered piles of robotic equipment, complete with tubes of viscous liquid and wicked metallic spikes.

Hector's voice startled Ash when he broke the silence. "Are these robot suits?" Hector asked.

Ash poked the closest one. It collapsed in a noisy

mess. The blackened bones of a long-dead mech pilot tumbled out.

"How did he drive it?" Hector asked.

Ash peered at the skull. Gold nodules sank through the bone. "Neurocontrols like Victor had for his kraken." She looked at Hector. "Why? Looking to pilot one of these?"

A shudder shook his big shoulders. "Not if I would need to get a machine in my head. No thanks."

"We can come out here tomorrow at nightfall with the rest of the team. This seems like what we're looking for, and we should have the other here just to be safe."

"That's very responsible of you, Ash."

"Shut up."

"I thought for sure you'd want to venture into the obviously dangerous zone. Maybe your brain has been taken over by nanomachines." Hector waved a hand in front of her face. "Should I call you Ashbot?"

"Shut up." She mock punched him on the arm.

Hector faked injury, staggering away. "Ow, Ashbot is super strong! She can't be stopped."

Ash watched him with her most serious expression, which she successfully held for almost three seconds. Then, she broke out into a huge grin, raised her hands high in the air, and said in a robot voice, "Ashbot directive received. Destroy puny human."

She was just about to jump at Hector when something below clanked. It sounded like a much smaller version of the noise that had shook the entire city at dawn.

"What was that?" Ash said. Her heart hammering.

Hector whispered, "What have you done, Ashbot?"

Metal ground against metal, and the floor shook with an almost imperceptible hum. Ash stepped into the street and watched as the steel plates halfway up the pyramid lifted. Air rushed through the streets, as if the pyramid were a giant inhaling a deep, long breath.

"It's almost morning," she said.

And all the tentacles in the area twitched.

"We should get back," Hector said. Oh, yeah, he was scared now. Ash was *definitely* going to need to comfort him.

"Are we too late?"

Hector chewed a lip.

"Maybe there's another way." They hadn't seen the tentacles wake before, so if they could get closer before stepping into the street they might be able to get back. Ash led Hector to a narrow staircase inside the biolab.

Hector froze at the top of the stairs. "We don't know where that goes."

"Sure, we do. It goes back. We can get to a street closer to the camp."

"We could wait here for the day."

"Or we could explore these totally safe underground ruins." Below, the lights activated, flaring to life to beckon Ash forward.

"What happened to being responsible?" Hector mumbled as he followed.

"I'm *always* responsible," Ash said at the bottom of the stairs. "Come on, let's explore these creepy ruins."

The explosion that had torn apart much of the lab had devastated the stairs and ravaged the floor below. The lights down below flickered to life, revealing walls of glassy obsidian. "This could be exactly what we're looking for."

"You know," Hector said, ducking to avoid hitting his head on the ceiling, "I think you suffer from a debilitating amount of curiosity."

"I wonder if Gerald can make ocelots."

"I can still tell when you're deflecting, and I don't even know what an ocelot is."

Ash opened her mouth to unleash the grand-mother of all deflections but closed it again when she saw what lay beneath the science lab. She pulled the paper map from her pack and consulted it.

The air smelled of ozone and ash, and the flickering hum of intermittent lights stretched into a long open space. Slick, black pods sat in rows, each festooned with tentacle-like tubes and shaped like sarcophagi. Closest to the stairs, the pods were cracked and broken, and the bodies they had once contained spilled out upon the broken floor.

"It's the colonists. Dead," Hector said, in awe.

Ash pointed down the row where the tunnel continued into the dark. "Let's look."

Hector didn't follow.

"It'll be fine," Ash said, waving the map. "It should take us closer to the others."

He pointed back the other direction, where a cave-in blocked the passage. "I think that's the direction back."

"It'll circle around." Ash infused her words with more confidence than she really felt. "If it doesn't, we'll just go back up the way we came down."

Their footsteps echoed in the vast space, and the wind howled above. The day's storm had come, and the clang rattled Ash's bones, even through the insulation of the stone tomb. Each pod they passed was progressively less damaged, but the bodies they contained were in various states of desiccation.

"Are we going under the pyramid?" Hector asked.

"They don't decay," Ash said, poking one of the bodies, "because Sky doesn't have the biological mechanism for it yet. They just dry out."

Hector touched one of the pods, coming away with a thick layer of gray dust.

They came upon a circle of sarcophagi, all standing on end, as if each stood vigilant, even in afterlife. The room, cloaked in oppressive black, stood at the nexus of a dozen branching corridors. Each pod held a tablet mounted to its front, and as Ash approached the closest, the screen blazed to life.

Strange symbols displayed on its surface, including a black variation on the Traverse logo.

Hector held his arms out as if to judge their distance. "We're definitely under the pyramid now. Ash, I don't think we should—"

"Traverse?" Ash said to the tablet.

The screen flickered once, then died. She tapped it, but it no longer responded. It felt loose on its mounting, and after a few tries, she detached the device and tucked it into her backpack.

In response to Hector's worry, she said, "This is for research purposes."

"We're not supposed to be here," Hector whispered. "Victor said it was dangerous."

"All the best research is dangerous." Victor hadn't said anything about going *under* the pyramid, but she didn't think that line of argument would work very well with Hector.

At the center of the circle stood a plinth containing two pods. One, the larger of the two, was cracked down the middle. Its black shell shone in places like melted glass, and the contents were all ash and metal. Peering through the gaping hole, Ash saw shining bits of conductive cord and a vicious spike amongst the charred spinal column of the burned corpse.

"What the heck is that?" she wondered aloud.

Hector said, "Maybe this is a cryogenics system."

"I don't see any signs of refrigeration."

"Pyrogenics?" Hector asked, a hint of amusement

edging out the fear. "Preservation of human life via cleansing flame."

"That doesn't sound like it would work very well at all."

"A lot of people think cleaning the atmosphere using flying microbes won't work either."

"Good point."

The hammer struck again. This time the floor shook so hard Ash felt it in her knees. Somewhere directly above, metal scraped against metal. The dark corridors leading away from the circular room hissed with movement.

A flash of metal at the base of the plinth caught Ash's eye—something small. She waited. Watched.

Nothing. The hissing stopped. Her heart thundered in her ears.

"What were you saying about leaving?" she whispered.

The second pod on the plinth hummed with energy. The obsidian tablet slotted into the front of this pod flickered with green light but went blank when Ash touched it.

Hector frowned at the sarcophagus. Using his sleeve, he scrubbed the dust from a viewing window to peer inside. He stretched as tall as he could and used his sleeve to wipe a layer of grimy dust from the window.

His eyes went wide.

The hammer hit so hard dust fell from the ceiling and Ash had to catch herself.

The lights around them flared, brighter and stronger than daylight. Tiny creatures scurried into the shadows. Their metal carapaces glinted in the unsteady light. Ash took Hector's hand and pulled him farther through the tomb. "It's time to go."

"Ash," he said. "That pod—"

Lights flashed bright again, and the single functioning sarcophagus on the plinth became a searing halo of light. The world around them buzzed with energy. Ash's heart raced. Where was the way out? She was turned around.

Then, insects swarmed. Hoppers fluttered into the air, their metal wings flashing in the light of the flaring sarcophagus. A menacing buzz filled the air.

"Run!" Ash shouted.

Together they raced through the passage. They passed strange clusters of writhing tentacles that grasped at their ankles. Hector jumped past the first and stomped the second so Ash could pass unhindered.

This wasn't the way they'd come. This was a new passage. They had no choice, though, but to continue. An insect landed on Hector's sleeve. He swore and swatted it away, blood darkening his shirt.

Light up ahead. She raced up a sand-covered set of stairs into the ruins of an old building.

Ash peered into the sand-filled street. "This way!" she shouted. Not far, the door to the entryway stood closed against the morning storm.

She covered her face with her scarf. Hector did

the same. Wind howled, pulling sand into a furious vortex around them. Holding Hector tight, she pulled him toward the camp. She could hardly see through her goggles. "Just a little farther!"

Metal insects—locusts—landed around them, flashing blue-black eyes in the hazy light. Ash kicked them away, swinging her backpack to sweep away dozens of them. Hector snatched one from her neck in his big hand, only to let it go again, his hand bloodied.

They hit the door. Behind them, in the ferocious static of the growing sandstorm, a band of metal halfway up the pyramid moved in the morning light. The building drew a huge breath through open vents. Ash heaved the door open and pushed through into a pocket of quiet in the onslaught of noise.

Juliette rushed to her, brushing at Ash's robes. "You don't have any on you, do you?"

"We're clear," Hector breathed. "Where are the others?"

Palak lay on one of the bedrolls. A cut ran along her forehead, and she clutched her ribs in both hands.

Juliette said, "Seth and Harish aren't back yet."

Hector bled profusely from his hand. Juliette rushed over with a bandage.

"How did Palak get hurt?" Ash asked.

"Those bugs. Palak got tired of waiting for her brother and went out to look. I'm just now bandaging her up, but there's some kind of poison. I don't think it's fatal, but I can't handle that here. I need a full med support system."

Ash swallowed her panic. The pinch on her elbow hadn't broken skin, but Hector and Palak were both injured. "They'll find shelter. It's what we should have done. We can find them again tonight."

Hector leaned against the wall, his face sallow. "Ash."

"Stop it," Ash said. "We just need to be patient. Nobody's dying on this trip. I'll walk through the storm to get the spider if I need to."

Juliette said, "We can't bring tech—"

"We'll bring it if we have to get Palak and Hector out of here. And we've already gone outside during the day."

Juliette checked a sheet of paper. "Traverse is rising now, so you were probably fine."

"Okay." Hector's breaths came in deep gulps. "Okay."

Seth burst through the door in a furious torrent of sand. He dropped to his knees and looked up at the others with a hollow expression.

"He's dead," Seth said between gulps of air. "Harish is dead."

Hector collapsed.

That night, with a pack of water and as much protective gear as she could manage, Ash, alone, set out to fetch Hector's spider. She ran all that night until her legs burned and every joint screamed for mercy. The Pyramid road stretched into the twilight, gray clouds of dust hazing the horizon. She ran until the winds started and walked until she could walk no more.

Then, finally, she came upon the spider.

She picked them up at the first pylon. Hector and Palak still lay unconscious, Seth wouldn't speak, and even Juliette wore a grim expression as she helped load their poisoned partners into the abdomen.

Ash's trip had finally gone horribly awry, and, as was the case with so many scientific expeditions before, it ended conclusively with dismal and unmitigated failure.

CHAPTER FOUR

"'It wasn't so bad,' I told the council," Ash said, sitting on the edge of her bed while Hector listened. "'If you think about it, our trip was a smashing success, scientifically,' I said. 'We discovered the location of the city, took some copies of their writing, and ended up with some really good questions to answer next time.'"

Hector groaned, but it wasn't directed at her comment. He was still in pain from the poison, the long ride home, and several days of medical treatment. He was recovering, but slowly. Too slowly.

Ash was doing a terrible job of taking care of him, but it was possibly his fault because he complained too much.

He whined every time she either touched him or did not touch him. He lay there useless while she scurried around to bring him whatever might make him more comfortable, but he refused to *be* comfortable. Didn't he even know how this was supposed to work? He rolled around in a state of semi-consciousness, kicking over the lamp and knocking a stack of books off the end table.

"I didn't say it was an unmitigated success," Ash explained. "And I explained to them that we broke Victor's rules. Victor grumbled a lot, but wouldn't say why it mattered, so I'm just going to ignore him."

He swatted the lamp, but she caught it this time.

She was doing a terrible job taking care of Hector, but it was probably her house's fault.

Her house was designed for *her*. As it should be. She wasn't a big person. Not tiny by any measure—well, maybe by *some* measures, but Hector was huge! He'd been there before, of course. He never seemed to mind that he couldn't stand all the way up or that his head and feet both touched walls when he lay down in the bedroom. She'd never heard any complaints before, but now every inconvenience irritated him, and the complaints were almost as relentless as his apologies for those complaints.

"Sorry," he said. "I always complain about stuff like this, but really, I'm feeling better."

Mr. Floofers, the fluffiest guinea pig, sat atop the big man's belly, rising and falling with his slow breaths.

Ash knew Hector well enough that his words meant very little. He almost always said he was fine. He rarely spoke honestly about his own pain. For that perfectly logical reason, Ash adopted a purely scientific approach to his care. She placed a warm cloth on his head because the medical tech said it might help with the aches.

"Ow," he said, swiping the cloth away. "That's too hot."

Ash checked the decibel meter attached to the headboard. This complaint wasn't his loudest by any means. Hardly midrange. She slapped an ice pack on his forehead.

"Ahh!"

Much louder. She tried another warm cloth. Grudging silence. Perfect. She made a note with her pencil and paper, quantifying her results with temperature and decibel notes. She would get better at this.

Ash was doing a terrible job taking care of Hector, but it was probably Simon's fault.

"Palak is getting better now that the poison is out of her system," Simon said when he stopped by. "She's up and walking around. Says she feels awful, but most of that's because she lost her brother."

"Thanks for the reminder." She handed Mr. Floofers to him.

Simon set Mr. Floofers down in the maze and advanced the automated feeding unit. When he stood, he knocked his head on the doorjamb. Why did she live amongst such giants? Simon wasn't even very tall, and he still stooped in her house.

"How are you doing, man?" Simon asked, kneeling next to Hector.

"He's fine," Ash said. "I just fed him a *lot* of soup."

"Still terrible, actually," Hector said. "Pretty much hurts everywhere."

Simon glanced at the bandages on Hector's wounded hand. "They tell me your body processes the poison differently from Palak. Much slower, but it'll get out of your system eventually."

"I wish it would hurry up. Feels like I'm swimming in molasses."

"It's some kind of sedative effect. Causes you to go dormant on a cellular level."

"Causes headaches is what it does." Hector peeled back white cloth to show off his cleaned wound on his hand. "How are those kids of yours?"

This brought a smile from Simon. "Vicious."

"They get that from Olympia," Ash said as she programmed the food printer to produce tea. She thought of Skye and how he'd been as a baby. After the business with his mother, he'd grown fast and strong, and his sharp teeth had only grown sharper. "Have they hit the climbing phase yet?"

Simon's eyes went wide. "Climbing?"

"Need a drink?" She tapped a bottle of green nectar.

"You know," Simon said, "I didn't sign up for this."

"We're aware," said Hector with a wry grin. "But you delegated your right to sign up for things when you fell for Olympia."

Simon dropped into Ash's best comfy chair. "But why triplets? Wouldn't it make more sense to have one or two at first? I mean, they outnumber us."

"You need to run a zone defense," Hector said from the other room.

"What the heck is that?"

Ash knew this one. "It's a sports reference, Simon."

"Sports. They're going to want to play sports."

Hector said, "If you can get Olympia to crank out a couple more real quick you might be able to field your own basketball team when they're older."

Simon gave Hector a blank stare.

"You know, they're rebuilding the gaming hall up by the Commons," Hector said, sitting up on his bed. "I bet we could add courts for basketball and tennis. Your kids'll love it."

Simon closed his eyes for a long time, breathing deeply. Ash wondered if he had come over simply for the respite. Finally, he said, "No, I think I'll pass on the drink. I have work to do back at the Archives and if I start drinking, I'm not ever going to stop."

"We could play another game of chess," Ash said. "I'm feeling pretty lucky."

"It's not a game of chance, Ash."

"Says the guy who's always lucky."

Ash was terrible at taking care of Hector, and it was probably because being near him when he was sick was the hardest thing she had ever endured, and that included catching that case of boils from Simon.

"Hey, how about if I come with to the Archives," she said to Simon, grasping at the excuse to take a break.

He gave her a pitiable, exhausted look, but nodded assent.

Once Hector was settled back into Ash's little bed, she picked up her backpack and found the dusty black tablet she had taken from Pyramid. With all the health problems and flurry around their arrival back home, she hadn't had time to do much with it. It wouldn't power up enough for her to even attempt to extract information. She kissed Hector on his sweaty, gross forehead and walked with Simon toward the Archives.

Outside, Ash squinted against the harsh afternoon sun. She hadn't been outside in days, having alternated her time between poorly tending to Hector and feeling bitterly, guiltily resentful for it. When, finally, her eyes adjusted to the light, she felt the odd sensation of stepping into a world that was painfully, irrevocably normal. It grated against her like an ill-fitting pressure suit.

Halfway up the slope, Skye ran past at full speed, his caretakers following as best they could. He outpaced them by half, and when they almost cornered him, he scrambled up the side of a building and disappeared over the top.

"You're doomed," Ash said to Simon. "Absolutely doomed."

"You should visit Palak," he said.

"Nope."

He stopped in the middle of the street. "What do you mean, 'Nope?'"

Ash set her jaw. "Her brother is dead from my mission."

"It's not your fault."

"I led them into danger. I was the one who thought everything would turn out fine when we poked that monster of a city." Simon started to talk, but she cut him off. "I made every decision that led to his death, and it was my call to not even search for his corpse."

"You had Palak and Hector to think about."

"And myself," Ash said so quietly she wasn't sure he heard it. "I was afraid for myself."

"You made the right choice."

"What good is that," Ash snapped. "One right choice after a series of bad ones doesn't make things good again. It makes everything bad, in fact." She thought of Hector still recovering on her bed. "Everything's worse after this, and the thing is I have no idea what I could have done better."

"You can only try to do better in the future," he said. "Go, apologize. Palak understands."

"I wouldn't if I were her. I'd be furious, and I'd probably plot terrible revenge on whoever killed my brother whether it was incompetence or malice."

"It wasn't incompetence."

"It wasn't malice. Anyway, I'm too busy to visit Palak." Ash thought of the screen she'd stolen from the ruins. "I need to see if I can get any value out of our one treasure."

Simon made a grand gesture up the road at the Archives. The building shone like a star on the hilltop, its reflective panels catching the afternoon sun. "Well, my friend, welcome to my place of employment, where we're happy to help so long as you agree to lend us your soul."

"I don't like the sound of that."

"The Archives are a sacred space, Ash. This is like how old Earth people had churches."

"Does that make you a priest?"

"More like a priest in training."

"I thought you were the guy in charge over there."

"That... has never been true."

"Do you have magic powers?"

"There have never been any magic powers, Ash."

A pair of guinea pigs scurried over Ash's feet. "There was once a monk who could talk to animals."

"That's not true."

"They called him Saint Francis and he was reincarnated as Doctor Dolittle."

Simon scowled.

"Possibly Doctor Who. Crack a book sometime, Simon. Then, maybe you would know some of this stuff."

Ash knew that Simon was considering her wise words carefully because he refused to speak for the remainder of their walk uphill to the Archives. When they arrived, Ash only thought one thing:

She was terrible at helping Hector because she wasn't there.

And the guilt only gnawed at her more when she stepped inside the round building and breathed the dry, electric air of the most sacred place she had ever been.

CHAPTER FIVE

THE ARCHIVE WAS a hollow nail driven into hard stone, with only a single large floor above ground and countless dozens below. The brutally angular roof of the round building sat at an odd angle, tilted to better catch the rays of the blue sun. Solar captures on its roof reflected the rays of the blue sun and cast them aside as a web of skewed rainbows.

"I'm afraid I'm going to have to ask you to leave, Miss Morgan," said Moira, the head Archivist. "Again."

"I'll be better this time," Ash said. "I promise."

Before Moira could respond, Simon said, "I'll keep an eye on her, Mrs. Heartell."

Moira was a white-haired woman with smooth skin that spoke of youth and a hard gaze that hinted at great age. She stood a full head shorter than Ash, but still always managed to look down on her. Whenever Ash visited the Archives that tightly bound bob of white hair followed relentlessly, always expecting trouble.

Not that Ash was allowed in the Archives anymore.

Ash said, "I have a directive from the science committee."

Moira scowled, but allowed them to pass.

The Archive was one of the few buildings in Edge that extended downward into solid stone rather than upward toward the sky. Presumably, this was so that it might better protect its most valuable asset: knowledge. The main core of the building continued the nail theme as a straight steel shaft plunged into rock flanked by a double-helix staircase. At regular intervals along the stairs, steel doorways led outward into rooms hewn from the surrounding stone. At the center of the shaft, an elevator granted access to anyone who didn't want to walk the hundreds of steps.

Moira blocked Ash's way to the elevator, arms crossed in front of her white blouse. "You'll take the stairs." When Ash started toward the closest entrance to the spiral, Moira shook her head. "The other stairs."

Ash looked at the sign, clearly marking it as the exit. "It goes to the same—"

"Stop," Simon said, placing a hand on Ash's shoulder. "We'll take the other stairs."

When they had passed through the scanner at

the top of the long spiral staircase, Ash said, "You know, things were just fine before she arrived."

"That's not even close to true."

"She's just like all the other newcomers. All full of themselves just because they qualified on some test somewhere."

"Ash, that's exactly how you feel about yourself."

"I scored *really* well on the test."

"So did everyone. Otherwise, they wouldn't be here."

"There's just so many of them. The biolab added an extension and it's already full. Even Gerald's guinea pig factory had to be moved off site."

"That was more out of a consideration for the smell."

Ash hadn't thought of that, but it was probably true. The guinea pigs did tend to stink. The muscles of her legs already burned from walking down stairs. They passed a steel door labeled "Fiction, Classics."

Simon elbowed her. "Remember when you tried to burn the Archive's paper copies of the Danielle Steel collection?"

Ash's mouth went dry. "I was proving a point."

"Which was?"

"That you shouldn't store classics on paper. It's too vulnerable."

"The fire suppression system worked, though."

Ash scoffed. "Almost killed me, you mean."

"Fire doesn't burn without oxygen."

"Yeah, neither do I."

"It's your own fault."

"Again, I was proving a point. They shouldn't print classics on fire bombs." She felt heat rise to her face. She really hadn't expected the books to ignite so easily—she hadn't expected any consequences; she just hated romance novels—but the elevated oxygen levels in the atmosphere meant everything was a fire hazard. "Plus, I was drunk."

"Did you ever figure out why Moira expelled you from the Archives?" Simon asked.

"It's a mystery," said Ash. "Look, I'm just here to get an opinion on this tablet."

"What tablet?"

Ash sighed. "There isn't anything in the connected records about the language I saw in Pyramid, and there isn't any way for me to find what information is stored on the thing without intentionally connecting it to Traverse's network. Plus, the battery's broken."

Simon stopped on the third floor down, which was marked *Fallen Nations*. "What tablet are you talking about, Ash?"

"Didn't I already tell you?"

"Ash."

She shrugged off her backpack and drew out the black tablet. The screen was dark, and the sand-scratched glass caught the harsh white of the overhead lights. "I picked it up from Pyramid."

Simon made an exasperated sigh, as if she'd done

something wrong. "There's an expert for stuff like this, Ash."

"Really?"

"Yeah. It's Moira."

Moira was the last person Ash wanted to deal with. "Can you call her?"

"There's no signal down here."

Ash's legs ached. "How about if you run up and get her." Ash could tell from his expression that this wasn't going to work. "Fine." She started walking up the stairs.

"Not that way."

"What?"

"We have to cross to the other side of the double helix. This side is only for going down."

"Be a rulebreaker, Simon."

Simon was not a rulebreaker.

Near the top of the stairs, Ash's messages pinged on her comm. She swiped through them on her screen, surprised that they would come all at once. "Is there really no signal down there?"

"Not past the first level. The farther down the more insulated it gets."

"Huh."

Hector had written. He was fine. The biolab had sent results from an experimental gut microbe that was going to allow guinea pigs to consume new varieties of grass. It caused the guinea pigs to bleed from their eyes, but failures are perfectly fine in science.

Not super frustrating or terrifying at all. Ash swiped her comm unit closed and stowed it in a pocket.

Moira was no longer at the top of the Archives by the time they defeated the stairs. Another worker pointed them to the fiction archives, so Simon and Ash once again descended.

Ash said, "We would have run into her if we had gone up the wrong spiral."

"Maybe that's why she doesn't want us to do that."

"How does it feel having a new arrival as a boss?"

"This isn't some competition like you scientists have going on in the lab. We all have parts to play in these archives. Our own areas of expertise."

"Like arranging story contests?"

"Culture isn't always about reliving the past."

"When is the next contest anyway? I think I have a good story about a brilliant scientist and her insufferable friend walking up and down stairs forever."

When they finally found Moira, she was behind the second steel door, surrounded by an exquisitely crafted server farm. Rows of databanks spiraled into the room, forming a kind of meditative labyrinth designed for contemplation and silence.

"We need your help," Ash called across the tops of the databanks.

Simon shushed her. "I told you," he whispered, "this is like religion."

"I don't know anything about religion."

"Religion is believing in something bigger than

yourself, even if you can't quite figure out what that is."

"I'm using that quote in my story."

Moira eventually found her way out of the labyrinth and approached the pair. "What is it?" She didn't slow as she passed them, and they had to fall in line behind her as she made her way around the databanks along the outer wall.

"Simon thought you could help with a tablet I found." Ash held out the device.

Moira looked at it like it might bite. "Is it broken?"

"A little."

"I don't fix tablets." Moira turned to continue her task.

Simon said, "Ash found it at the Pyramid colony. We thought you might help us discover what information is on it."

Moira stopped in her tracks, not turning around to speak. "You'll leave it with me."

"No," Ash said, "I just need you to—"

Moira spun on Ash. "This device will stay down here in the Archives. To take it up above would be to risk everything."

"I—"

Simon placed a hand on Ash's shoulder to stop her from saying something stupid.

It didn't work. "It's not staying in your stupid archive because I need information off of this to save our planet." Ash held the tablet up high where Moira couldn't easily grab it. Wow, being tall was such a power trip. "If you can help me decipher Pyramid's language, then I'll let you help. If not, I'm leaving."

Moira clenched her fists. "We have a languages room."

"Where's that?" Ash asked Simon.

"All the way down to the bottom."

They followed Moira downward. Despite her short legs, Moira moved along the stairs as if a few hundred steps one way or another was nothing to her. Ash's legs had an entirely different opinion.

"Mrs. Heartell and the other new colonists always knew that there were other colonies," Simon explained. "Part of their faith in Traverse has to do with the spread of information, so this tablet of yours might be considered sacrilege."

"Oh, thanks. Now you tell me." Ash thought about it for a moment. "So, as soon as we figured out that there were other colonies, Traverse started sending us people who already knew?"

"That's about right."

Ash leaned against the outer wall, letting Moira get ahead by a few more paces. "Do they know that Traverse sometimes murders entire civilizations?"

Simon said, "Was Pyramid destroyed by Traverse?"

Ash thought about it. The technology there was strange and foreign. The sandstorms and locust robots were dangerous, especially during the day, but those weren't necessarily ways that the AI would have tried to kill everyone, especially when a beam from the sky seemed fairly effective. Rushing down the stairs to catch up to Moira, she said, "I need you to help me justify another trip to Pyramid."

"Don't take the next step until you've finished the last," Moira said.

"That is *not* how I live my life."

Moira stopped at the seventh door, which had no label at all. She unlocked it with a physical key she kept on a band around her neck. The door creaked as it opened, howling its protest into the vast dark above. Ash felt the weight of hundreds of tons of heavy rock above their heads. The tunnels down this low were dark, and beyond the massive door, no lights shone at all.

"Come along," Moira said.

Ash stepped into the dark, using her comm unit to shine a dull glow into the inky black. It didn't help at all, except to show her that the floor in front of her was decorated with an intricate grid. Each panel contained a stylized 'T', much like the logos that spun while Traverse was computing particularly difficult problems. In the center of the room sat an empty steel table.

"Set the tablet on the table," Moira said.

Ash complied, unsure what other options she might have. When she did, the door behind them closed without so much as a whisper.

On the table, Moira placed a battery lamp that washed the room in sterile white light. The walls lacked databanks or servers but contained rows of metal racks. Vertically stored steel sheets stood by the thousands.

"Records of our knowledge," Moira said, seeing Ash's interest. "Etched into metal and made impervious against electromagnetic interference, fire, or most any natural disaster. It might even survive an earthquake, though digging them out would still be a chore."

"Why?" Ash asked before she could stop herself.

"Because this is our duty, just like you've been asked to develop organisms that might shape this planet, we're asked to store knowledge that might shape our future civilizations."

Simon pulled a metal slide from the shelf so that Ash could see the intricate etchings on them. "It's no less important, Ash. And it's not easy."

It was definitely less important, but Ash applied her tremendous willpower and prevented herself from saying it. "Sure, Simon," she said. "Sure." It might have sounded sarcastic, but one can really only expect willpower to take things so far. "So, how does that help?"

Moira fished a conversion rig from a bin along one wall and used it to plug her battery lamp into the tablet. After matching the Traverse logo to a series of metal translation slates, she pulled one free and set it on the table next to the tablet. "This will take some time," she said.

Ash crossed her arms. "I'll wait." She placed her paper copies of the Pyramid language on the table.

"Ash," Simon said, "I think I recognize some of this. We can probably translate."

"How long will that take?"

Moira gasped. "This is the language used by only the most dangerous colonies. These colonies originated before wisdom taught our people moderation. They delved into dangerous technologies forbidden those who live now. These technologies broke the people who used them."

Ash asked, "Can you really trust what Traverse says?"

Moira looked up sharply. "Sometimes we have no choice."

"You can't be serious," Ash said.

Moira pointed at the translation slate on the table, which showed the same strange text Ash had copied down. "Translate it yourself."

It took Ash an embarrassingly long time to decipher the few lines of text. At first, she thought there were no letters, as the symbols blended into one another. Then, she figured out the tendency of the language to use large, complex symbols for words, but individual letters as modifiers. It all seemed need lessly complex, and all the time she worked on it, Simon and Moira discussed the situation in harsh whispers just past the edge of her hearing.

Of course, she didn't ask for help. She was definitely smart enough to do this kind of work.

"I got it," she said tentatively after far too long. "I think."

"What does it say?" asked Moira, an infuriating hint of amusement in her voice.

"It says, 'Entombed here lies the wisdom of the dead. To fear is to live. To follow is to die. Delve deeper and risk damnation.'" She peered at it one last time to be sure her translation was correct. "Well, that's cheery, isn't it?"

"Are you sure you want to know what's on this tablet?" Moira asked.

Ash nodded.

"I'll begin an indexing, Simon will brush up on this language, and you can visit when we have something useful."

"You're giving me back my Archive access?"

"As long as you promise not to burn anything." She pursed her lips. "And you will be escorted at all times."

Ash made no such promise, but Simon led her up the long, long spiral out. He didn't speak a word the entire trip up, but Ash couldn't tell if that was because he was out of breath or thinking too hard about the tablet's warnings.

"It'll be useful," Ash said as they approached the top. "I promise we'll be responsible with what we learn."

"Ash, I've never known you to be responsible with any knowledge ever."

"But this'll be different." That sounded twice as

sarcastic as she had intended. "I promise." That too. "I *totally* promise." Much better.

Ash emerged into the top level of the archives, and her comm unit pinged with several messages. Hector was fine. The biolab had more results. Hector was fine. The Commons had a new variety of nectar. Hector was fine.

Palak wrote with a curious message. *Ash, come inside already.*

I can see you out there by the rocks.

Come on, Ash, just get over here already.

Palak's messages continued for a while until finally, the last one:

Fine, I'm coming out there. We have to talk.

Then, for the past several hours, Palak wrote nothing.

CHAPTER SIX

PALAK LIVED upslope from the Commons, in one of the clusters of housing created for the newest waves of colonists. As visitors from Anvil, Palak and Harish had been issued one of the houses at the very edge. The settlement consisted of rough printed stone buildings arranged in a twisted maze, each in a different pastel. Palak's was a hazy teal with pink frill around the windows.

Ash pulled her rebreather close to her face. The air tasted exceptionally dusty. Wind pulled swaths of gray grit across the cobblestone streets, and the sky turned from white to slate. People in the streets huddled close and kept to themselves.

She turned a corner and saw a figure on the rise overlooking Palak's neighborhood. A big man. A silhouette in the late day's last light.

"Harish?" she said, but she knew she was wrong the moment she said it. Harish was dead.

Hector turned to look at her, a grim frown on his pale face.

"Why are you here?" Ash asked.

"Palak wrote." Hector pointed to the north. "Then I saw that."

The sky over the mountain peaks was a black haze.

"What is that?" Ash said.

"The desert," Hector whispered. "With the black sand."

He was acting strange, and Ash couldn't understand why. "You shouldn't be out here."

"It's coming for me." He stared into the distance. "I can feel it in the ache in my bones. It's coming to take me back."

Ash took his arm and forced him to look at her. "Is that a sandstorm? We need to warn people." If the storm hit as hard as it had in the desert, it would be dangerous. A smudge was rolling over the farthest mountains, but Ash, not knowing how far away they were, couldn't gauge how close the storm was.

She drew out her comm unit and remembered the messages from Palak. There weren't any new ones. Where had she gone? "Did you find Palak?" she asked Hector as she punched in a message to Orson back in the Commons building. He would know how to raise an alarm about the storm.

Hector shook his head.

Ash made a frustrated noise as she typed. Her

signal glitched. "Why don't we have a colony-wide alert system?"

Hector blinked. The oddness drained from his expression, replaced by a warm smile. "We do."

"Then why didn't anyone tell me about it?"

"We run drills every third Thursday night."

Ash mashed the send button again. Nothing. Frustration constricted her chest. The dark smudge on the horizon grew. "Shots and karaoke night?"

"Yeah."

"Palak went after someone. It wasn't me."

"Ash," said Hector, an unidentifiable note in his voice, "there's something I need to tell you."

"Why is the signal so bad here?" The wall of sand roared closer. She shook her comm as if that might jar it into a better signal.

Hector held her arm and waited for her panicked eyes to find him. "Ash. I saw you at the Pyramids."

"And I saw you." She tried to get someone—anyone—on a voice signal, but all she found was a hiss of noise. She swore and paced along the ridge. The signal had never had problems before.

"That's not what I mean." He ran his fingers through his hair, looking more tired than she'd ever seen him. "It keeps running over and over in my head. At first, I thought it might be some kind of fever dream brought on by the poison, but I don't think it was. As I heal, my memories sort themselves out."

"You had fever dreams? Any good ones?"

"Fever dreams aren't exactly known for fluffy clouds and dancing unicorns."

Ash stared at him. "You had a bad dream about me?"

He continued, "When we were under the lab at the center of it all, and you were messing with the tablet."

Ash opened her mouth to tell him the latest news on the tablet, but then she remembered the wall of sand coming their way and decided it might be best to let Hector say his thing. "We should move," she said, drawing him along, her comm unit extended as far into the air as she could manage.

He grabbed her shoulder and fixed her with a haunted look that poured ice on her spine. "It was you in there, Ash. In the sarcophagus. She looked just like you. Something Palak messaged reminded me of it. That's why I came out here. To find her, and to find you."

Ash stared into his eyes, waiting for him to crack into a smile. That wasn't Hector's sense of humor, though. "Do you think—do you think there's a clone of me?"

"Ash."

"No, you're right. The timing doesn't work. Maybe I'm a clone of her. But, I have two parents and all my DNA has well-documented provenance. Traverse is very careful about things like that."

"We need to find Palak."

Ash shook her comm unit again, which for some

reason still didn't help its signal. The sandstorm was definitely closer now, and if they didn't warn the colony soon there would be problems. "I even know who my genetic grandparents are. Met one of them once when I was really little. She was super old."

Hector took her comm and held it high in the air. The signal connected.

"I hate tall people," Ash said.

"You really don't, though." Hector handed back the unit. "We make wonderful pawns in your diabolical game."

Ash steepled her fingers and flashed him a wicked grin. "Indeed."

A long wail of a siren howled out to the colony from the Commons building.

"Bottoms up." A wave of relief washed over Ash. The storm still approached, but at least people would have a warning. "I'll find Palak. You go home."

He looked exhausted. "I can come with."

"Just go home," she said, turning him the right direction. "I'll take care of this."

"No, I—"

"Home," Ash commanded. "Now."

"You don't even know where she went."

Ash pointed at Palak's house. "She saw me outside her window. My clone must have been around those rocks, near the path."

Hector blinked at her. "You really think it's a clone from Pyramid? She followed us?"

"Maybe there are hundreds of Ashes out there

and we're genetically designed for a specific purpose, but you need to go home."

Hector said. "Someone should—"

"Look," she said, "You're worthless right now. I don't know how far off that storm is, but I can move faster on my own. You can stop by the reservoir and warn people on your way back if it makes you feel better." It all came out harsher than she had intended, but the hurt look in his eyes let her know the message got through.

"Thank you," he said. "For listening."

Ash kissed him on the cheek and shooed him away.

As he left, he said, "Just be careful," which was a ridiculous thing to say.

Ash was always careful.

Wind whipped at Ash's hair by the time she made her way along the mountain path behind Palak's house. Grasses grew from mud-packed corners along the granite trail, but every step fell on naked granite. This was a well-worn and clean path, and she saw no clear evidence that Palak had come this way. Sand, picked up by the stormfront's wind, swirled around in the protected space in the narrow space between boulders. The storm wall hadn't hit yet, but the sound of it roared in her ears.

Ash rushed forward, unsure how far she could go before the storm would turn her back. Her calves ached and her breath ran short.

She rounded a corner and ran straight into Palak. They collided. Collapsed.

Palak scrambled away, fear flashing in her brown eyes. "Get away!" She ran up and away, farther from the safety of her home. Wind crashed down the length of the path, driving sand and grit into Ash's face as she pursued.

"Palak, wait!"

She rounded another corner, and the path opened into a wide, flat expanse of clean stone. Ahead, she saw the wall of the sandstorm bearing down on them. Palak saw it, too, and froze against the backdrop of its enormity.

Ash said, "We need to go back to your house."

Palak met her gaze and the amber around her irises caught the light. "Is it really you, Ash?"

She gestured for Palak to return up the path. "We need to leave. That storm—"

But she couldn't finish the sentence, because she saw the woman at the edge of the storm. A woman with long, graying hair and dark goggles stood where the sandstorm raged its worst. She wore a cloak of the purest black over a tight outfit made of a matte material that tugged ruthlessly at the light around it. She walked like a huntress—a picture of confidence and power. Ash had no doubt that the storm belonged to this woman.

And the woman was Ash.

Or possibly an older spitting image of her. How, Ash didn't know, but she *had* to know.

The woman saw them and pointed a finger their direction. A flash of lightning arced across the sandstorm behind her, and in its light, Ash saw the reflective metal of a thousand robot insects. The woman flicked her wrist, and a blade of blue flame flared to life in her hand.

Ash decided she could learn more later. It was definitely on the to-do list. "Run!"

Palak bolted back down the path, and Ash followed as fast as she could. The wind that had buffeted her face before now shoved her in the back. She soared down the path, feet finding purchase on the scoured granite. She caught up to Palak, and the two reached the house at the edge of the settlement as the storm slammed into them.

Razor-sharp sand scoured the exposed parts of Ash's face and hands. She kept her eyes closed tight but lost her bearing. Wind pulled her from the house. A drop in air pressure popped her ears. The thunderous roar of wind blocked all other sound. She covered her face with her arms and felt flesh rubbing raw where it could find no cover.

Then, Palak's strong grip found her arm and pulled her inside the house.

The door slammed shut, and all the world became the wind-rushed roar and Palak's scrutinizing gaze.

"That was you out there," said Palak.

Ash shook the sand from her hair, wincing at the

abrasions on her arms and face. "I don't know who that was," Ash said, even though it was painful to admit it. "I don't know."

CHAPTER SEVEN

Nervous minutes passed with Ash peering out into the gray-black storm. The wind raged, but that woman didn't try to enter Palak's house.

Ash used Palak's shower to clean the grit from her skin and printed herself some new clothes. The old ones were ruined by her short time in the sand-storm, as was every painful square inch of exposed skin. After a stinging shower, she tended her wounds with an antiseptic spray-on bandage and dressed in a tight-fitting white outfit with an excess of buckles and zippers, covered by a long, white coat and matching gloves. She borrowed a pair of goggles and a head-wrap but didn't put them on.

Finally, feeling more human and properly dressed for the elements, she sat on Palak's best comfy chair and listened to the howling storm.

"Tea?" asked Palak.

"No, thank you."

Minutes passed.

"She looked just like you," Palak said.

Ash closed her eyes and pictured the woman in black. "She had gray hair."

"I just assumed it was a"—she waved a hand at Ash—"fashion thing."

"Gray hair is not a fashion thing. It's an old age thing. If she's my clone, then she's an older clone than me."

"You don't like what that implies."

Several more minutes passed. "I'm sorry about your brother."

Palak's expression hardened. "He didn't want to come."

Of course not. That made Ash feel way worse, so she said nothing.

"We were happy up on the ship, my brother and I, but I wanted adventure. We always did the same things every day. Explored the same parts of the ship."

"Yeah. Wander the city."

"More than that. We found hidden places. Secret entrances to things. We were good at it."

Ash leaned forward on her elbows. "You able to go places outside the habitat?"

Palak stared out the window. Sand still blasted against the glass. "Maybe Traverse was showing us places that it wanted us to discover." Her expression grew darker. "And I don't know what would have happened to us had we stayed."

"Traverse doesn't waste resources. If it thought you were worth bringing down, then it probably would have kept you alive for a future shuttle."

"Maybe."

"I guess there's no way to know." Ash swallowed the lump of guilt in her throat, wishing she had accepted the offer of tea. She looked at the Anvilite woman and saw how much she resembled her brother. The two had always been together before, so seeing her alone felt wrong. Finally, when the guilt threatened to choke her, Ash said, "I'm still sorry about Harish. Everything happened so fast."

Palak said nothing to this, but Ash knew what she must be thinking. They should have looked for Harish. They should have at least *tried* to save him the way they had saved Hector. It was Ash's fault the mission went wrong, and Ash's fault that they couldn't even properly mourn the loss of her brother.

"Have you talked to Seth?" Ash asked.

"When I was well enough to leave the medical center, I came here. I haven't had the energy to do anything else. It's so empty here."

The wind howled so loud their conversation had to stop. Eventually, when the noise died down, Ash said, "Juliette saved you, you know."

"I know."

"I mean, I told her to split our remaining meds between you and Hector. She wouldn't listen, and she was right. I shouldn't be the one in charge."

Palak's jaw tensed, and she said nothing.

———

THE STORM DIED like all things: gradually, and then with a suddenness that left a hole in the very air itself. Ash opened the door to a world covered in black sand and cloaked in a thick gray haze. They walked through the streets. Others emerged from their homes with blank stares and shuffling feet. Loose sand muted sound and put soft edges on hushed voices.

"We need to clean up," Orson said when they joined a group in the courtyard in front of the Commons, "but first we need to make sure everyone's accounted for." He held up a tablet. "Everyone get your instructions from me. Check your name off the list, then follow this grid to search for other survivors. Once we find everyone, we'll work on cleaning up sand and fortifying against another storm." He was the perfect leader. Calm, collected, organized. Everything Ash had never been.

Ash kicked at a particularly large swell of sand in the street and found it was formed around the skeleton of a guinea pig. The skull clattered to the cobblestones and stared up at her. Her heart pounded in her chest.

"Palak," she said.

"What?"

"Sandstorms don't do this."

Palak stared down at the skull, her mouth open in horror.

"I saw locusts in the sand cloud," Ash whispered.

Palak pushed through the crowd. She made her way to Orson grabbed a tablet and checked her and Ash's names off the list. Somewhere, someone cried.

"Palak, wait. We should talk about this."

"No," Palak said.

"Locusts stripped the flesh off a guinea pig."

"No!" Palak spun on her. "Harish is dead and now you're telling me he was picked clean like that pig. What would they do that for? Why take the flesh off someone like that?"

Ash couldn't think. "I don't know." Biomass, probably, but what for?

"Well, what do you expect me to do?" She held up the tablet. "Orson has us searching the lower quarter."

"I need to go to the reservoir."

"Why?"

Because it's where Hector would have gone if he didn't go home. "There might be people stranded. The alarms are harder to hear up there."

Palak shook her head. "We stick together." She broke from the crowd and entered the Commons building.

Ash followed into the dark and empty cantina. "I can head up alone. I'll be fine."

"Hector said..." Palak drew a deep breath. "This was an attack. We need to defend ourselves."

"She has a storm and a swarm of locusts. Whoever she is, we can't fight that."

Palak glanced above the bar, where the colony's only energy weapon sat in a sealed case. "If we can take her down—"

"What if we can't?"

Palak clutched a hand to her chest. Her breathing grew shallow and quick, her face pale. Gold flecks glinted as her panicked eyes darted from Ash to the tables and chairs around them, then back to Ash. "I don't know," she said.

Ash drew the girl close and hugged her like a comforting aunt. It seemed to work, and after a little while, Palak's calmed. They left the cantina and started toward the quarter Orson had designated for them.

"I want to go back," Palak said. When Ash glanced in the direction of Palak's house, the girl shook her head. "Not there. I want to go back to Pyramid. To find Harish or whatever's left of him."

Ash spotted another lump covered in the black sand. And another. Releasing Palak, she cautiously shuffled sand around to reveal what she suspected. More guinea pigs. Scattered in the corners where the drifts of sand formed makeshift dunes in the corners between buildings. Places where the wind would have been the least, the damage was the most. Little creatures, thousands of them, were scoured clean of flesh and fur. Their little skeletons lay in a quaint ossuary that would have been adorable if it weren't so disturbing, arranged in a tumbled mass at the base of each building.

"What is this?" Palak asked.

"Like you said. An attack," said Ash. "Or, possibly a plague of the apocalypse." She punched into Traverse's feed. "Traverse, what is the status of our food supply?"

Traverse made no reply.

"Hector," Ash said, trying to signal the big man again with her comm unit.

Nothing.

She checked her connection. No response. She pinged Orson. He pinged back immediately.

"I need to go to the reservoir," Ash said. "Then I need to check my house."

"You're worried about Hector," Palak said. "We go together, then."

On the way up the hill, they passed Juliette and Jasper. The pair had knocked on doors and checked off a dozen citizens, but there was still work to do, and they already looked exhausted. When Ash explained that she was going to check near the reservoir, Juliette nodded approval.

"There isn't much shelter up there."

"We can cover your square down here," Jasper said, sounding as tired as he looked. "But you owe me one."

If anyone were keeping track, Ash probably owed Jasper dozens by now, which was why it was good nobody kept track.

They were halfway up the slope when Ash saw Hector's black and red spider parked at an odd angle against the base of a large granite slab. Sand piled around the legs, drifting against the rock and swallowing half the machine in a wash of shadow and dust. As she approached, Ash saw the thousands of tiny scratches decorating the outside of the spider. The locusts had come for it. Followed it all the way back here.

A puff of dust rose into the air as Ash pulled open the cockpit door, blinding her. She staggered back and waved through the cloud.

Then, a cough from inside. Someone moved in the cockpit.

"Hector?" she asked, but as soon as she said it she knew it wasn't him.

Unsteadily, Seth climbed from the spider and landed on his feet with a thump.

Ash blinked. "Where's Hector?"

Seth pulled himself up and past her, climbing to the ground. "Thought I was done for."

"Where is he?"

Seth leaned up against the spider and removed his rebreather. Tapping it, he watched as a stream of fine dust puffed into the air, refracting rainbows in the afternoon light. His face was caked in muddy sweat. "Headed for the spider when the storm hit," he said. "Thought I'd get there in time, but the storm hit before I got it closed." He coughed hard and spat mud.

"Did he come up here?" Ash asked.

"He stopped by to check in," Seth said. "Then he went for shelter."

"Home?" The knot of anger tightened into an equal mix of rage and worry. If he hadn't made it—

Seth nodded. "I wasn't sure he'd get there, but he pinged me on the comm when he arrived."

Ash looked at the screen of her own comm. No messages from Hector. He must have gone home and crashed, which made sense if he was in such bad shape. Still... "I thought he would have pinged me too."

Seth brushed dust from his short hair and wiped sweaty mud from his tanned skin.

"You both abandoned Hector," Palak said. "Why does nobody know how to stick together?"

"Why would you say that?" Seth bristled before Ash had a chance to respond.

Palak stepped up into his face. "When you got a partner, you stick together through trouble."

Seth opened his mouth to say something else, but no words came out. Instead, he turned and stalked away up the stony path.

"You don't leave him," Palak whispered.

Ash looked to Palak, but the younger woman shrugged as if she'd done nothing wrong.

Hurrying up the path, Ash shouted, "Seth, wait."

He spun on her. "I told you he's in your house. He stopped by here, but he needed rest. Now, if you don't mind, I've got work to do. This town needs digging out."

"I believe you." It was almost the truth. "He was supposed to go straight home."

"He did," said Seth. "He got there. I promise."

Ash looked back at the half-buried buildings at the edge of town. There was too much work to do to worry about Hector. He was a capable man and always took care of himself. He needed rest, and that was the one thing she could do for him. That was the one aspect of caretaking that she could reliably provide. All she needed to do was stay away. "Where to first?"

Seth led her along the higher route, which would give them the better vantage point of the whole reservoir valley. Hand over hand, they climbed up the steep, rocky slope. Seth's work in Victor's compound kept him in good shape, and Ash gasped heavily as dust clogged the vents in her rebreather. She dared not remove it and couldn't stop to unclog the device, for fear of being left behind. Instead, she pushed forward, careful not to disturb more dust.

They mounted the top of the rise and stood overlooking the reservoir. Seth kicked at clods of sand. She couldn't see other survivors down below, but there weren't any bodies either. Maybe they had made it to shelter after all.

But the gray clouds shifted and sunlight hit the small lake.

"Ash," Seth muttered.

The reservoir was red as blood.

CHAPTER EIGHT

A LAKE RED AS BLOOD. Choking, toxic sand. Four colonists dead.

The round-faced boy who ran everywhere he went. The heavily muscled woman who worked up by the reservoir. The man with the ridiculously long mustache who probably worked in food service, but Ash didn't know for sure. The woman from Anvil who wanted so badly to have children. Dead. All four of them. Suffocated when they were caught without shelter.

Not scoured clean like so many guinea pigs she had found, but dead all the same. Suffocated in the freakish sandstorm that had struck so many miles from the desert. Funerals were planned for the next day. Ash dreaded each one. If only she had gotten the warning out earlier. If only she hadn't led danger back to the colony.

If only she hadn't broken Victor's rules.

"Do not bring technology close to Pyramid," Victor had said. Was this the consequence? "Do not enter the pyramid. Do not walk outside by day if Traverse is in the sky." Ash had broken every rule. Four colonists paid for her sins, and the guilt burned in her chest.

All around town, construction spiders built new wind barricades and cleaners swept black sand from the streets. Night had fallen, but the work of cleanup had only begun.

Then, there was the reservoir. It wasn't blood that tinted the water, but algae. Part of Ash desperately wanted to study it. Another wanted nothing more than sleep. Glorious sleep.

Hector's comm unit sat half-buried in dust on the path in front of her little house. She scooped it up on her way past. That explained why he wasn't answering.

Her place was dark when she shouldered her way through the door, so she moved quietly through the main room, careful not to shine any light near the sleeping compartment where Hector still slept. By feel, she located a copy of an Earth classic, printed on real paper and curled up on the comfy chair in a tiny halo of light. Sleep wouldn't come easy, despite the exhaustion aching in her bones. She wondered if she would ever be able to sneak the book back into the romance section of the Archives without Moira knowing. The truth was, Ash needed to read more of this book. She *hated* romance books so much for how demanding they were on her time, but what other options did she have?

After a few pages, she navigated her way through the dark until she located an unopened bottle of nectar, which greatly improved both her book and her mood.

"Cheers, Hector," she said, tipping the bottle back to take a big swig. Ash was a terrible caretaker because when she had something to say, she simply could not let the big guy sleep. It had taken her minutes of convincing and all her willpower to let him sleep off the afternoon. He needed it so badly. Now that she was home, she needed to talk. "I can't help but feel like the woman's here looking for something. Why else would she follow us here and pretend to be me? Does she want our tech?"

Hector didn't answer. In fact, he didn't make any noise at all, which bothered some remote corner of Ash's brain. She took another drink. Better.

"I mean, she might be here to wipe us out. Pyramid is an old colony, so it's possible it became overly aggressive in its later years." She took a pull of nectar. The burn in the back of her throat made the dark room spin. "With all the crap Traverse puts us through, I wouldn't doubt that at all." She looked up at the ceiling, even though Traverse's microphones were everywhere. "You hear that, Traverse, you turd?"

Traverse did not respond, and Ash did not appreciate the silence. She took another deep draw and slouched back into her chair.

"Well, I'm right anyway," she said. "She's looking for something, and the only thing we took from Pyramid was that stupid tablet. Well, she can have it."

Still, Hector didn't respond. Neither did Traverse. What the hell?

"I should go make sure she didn't actually take it." Another swig. "Tomorrow."

The minutes passed at an indeterminate pace, time itself tangled up in the darkness and the drink. Ash swelled with pride at having managed to get what she wanted while leaving the lights out so Hector could sleep. Pretty sneaky. She should organize a heist, and not just another brilliant raid on the romance section of the Archives. Something better. Something dangerous.

She looked up at the ceiling to talk to Traverse. "I'm getting pretty good at this," she said too loudly. "You know, I'm not the best caretaker, but if you haven't noticed, Hector's been getting better, so I must be doing something right. Rest is the key. Rest and good food. I can definitely run the food printer." She drank another swallow of nectar. "Med printers are a little tricky, though. Weird interface. Someone should fix that."

Her bottle hit the carpeted floor with a *thunk*. She picked it up before it sloshed too much on the floor.

"Definitely going to check on that tablet in the morning. If there's anything to learn about the mummy, it'll be on there."

She stopped and narrowed her eyes. Something she'd said had made more sense than she had expected. Then she figured it out.

"I hate monsters." No, that wasn't it.

Her legs wobbled as she stood, but it didn't bother her. She crossed her comfortable little house, shuffling so that she didn't trip over anything. When she reached the bed compartment, she slapped the covers so that she wouldn't accidentally fall on her big old boyfriend.

Only, her hand swept through empty space. Unbalanced, she sloshed nectar all over the bed.

The empty bed.

Ash flipped on the light. The bed was empty except for a rapidly emptying bottle of nectar and a slip of paper. She blinked at the paper, which contained Hector's blocky handwriting. *Ash, she's outside and she says the storm won't stop until I leave with her. It's the woman from the sarcophagus in Pyramid. I don't think I have a choice. I have to go. She won't kill me. She looks like you, Ash. Older, maybe. I'll be fine.*

Then, at the bottom, he sloppily scrawled: *She's not you.*

A pain stabbed Ash's heart. Her knees went weak, so she sat on the edge of the bed. He wasn't there. Hector had met the stranger and—what? Left with her?

She's not you.

What did that even mean? Of course, the stranger wasn't Ash. She was a clone or a doppelgänger or something. She could be anything, really.

Panic burned in Ash's chest. She wanted to stand, to rush after him and wrestle him from whoever had taken him. Was he really gone? Her head spun with the possibilities. That might have been the nectar. She needed answers.

She needed help.

"Folks who saw her said she was like your ghost," said Orson. Late into the night, and the bartender still organized cleanup and defense crews. "Everyone who spotted her in that storm said she looked like you, but gray."

"Will you send anyone with me to track her down?" She glanced at the case behind the bar where Marta's old energy weapon had been just hours earlier. The case was empty. "Did Palak take the weapon?"

Orson had the decency to look abashed. "You'll have to ask around for people willing to go with you."

"Can't you order people to help?"

He gestured with open palms. "That isn't how this works."

"The weapon?"

"Seth." Orson drew a long breath, and the bags

under his eyes deepened. "You might have some luck asking him."

Seth tossed a bundle into the back of a small one-person walker. "I don't know what that woman is, but something weird is going on and I'm not waiting for you to figure it out."

"We can go together," Ash said. "It'll be safer."

"Like last time?" Seth patted the knife casually strapped to his belt. "I've got my own troubles. I don't need yours."

"What are you talking about?"

He gestured at everything around them. "You messed up. This time I'm going on my own. If I run into Hector, I'll help him out. I don't need you along, and I don't need to wait for you to gather the rest of them yokels."

Anger burned the last of the nectar from Ash's veins. "This isn't my fault."

"I'm not here to place blame. I just want what's coming to me. What Victor sent you for that you failed to get."

"I don't know what you're talking about."

"The hell you don't," Seth snapped. His hand rested on the knife at his hip.

Ash's heart pounded and the air tasted of acid.

Seth looked down at the knife as if only then realizing it was there. "I'm going back," he said. "On my own."

"What happened with Harish, Seth?"

The man's neck muscles tensed under deeply tanned flesh. Instead of answering, he kicked at a clod of sand, sending a guinea pig skull skittering across the cobblestones. "I'm going back," he said, and he unclipped a canteen from his belt and took a long pull. "I don't care what they say. I want what's owed me." With that, he climbed into his walker and left.

Simon folded his arms and leaned against the doorframe to his modest two-story home. A trio of babies cried in the background. "She could be a version of you traveled back in time."

Ash scrunched her face. "You think I'll figure out time travel?"

"Oh, I sincerely hope not."

Olympia passed through the room behind Simon carrying two babies. "Nope!" she called. "No way. He's not going with you."

"I'll bring him back," said Ash. The nectar had long since burned off in the fury of her quest, but her exhaustion might have slurred her words.

"You don't have the best track record on that, girl," Olympia said.

Ash's face grew hot. "I brought back *almost* everyone last time."

Simon tried to placate them both with open palms, which did not work one bit. "You don't need me," he said.

Olympia handed a fussy baby to Simon. "You've been asking around town. Nobody's seen Hector and nobody wants to go with you immediately in the morning to chase after him."

"Do you want to go?" Ash asked Olympia.

Olympia paused, her mouth open. She looked down at the crying baby in her arms. "I'll think about it."

"You don't need either of us," Simon said. "If you're going to Pyramid, you need someone who can protect you."

"I need you to help me steal my tablet back from the Archives."

Simon hissed through his teeth. "Meet me there in a few hours. I need to help put the kids to sleep."

Ash opened her mouth to protest, but his words sunk in. "Really? You'll help me break in?"

"No, I..."

Backing away, Ash waved. "Thanks, Simon! You're a real friend!"

"I'm not going to..."

But she had already left.

"Human facsimile robot," said Leonard. Dust rained from his explosion of gray hair. "It's the only logical explanation."

"How is that logical at all?" asked Ash. "And why would they make her older-looking than me?"

Leonard narrowed his gaze at her. "Why, indeed," he mumbled. "Why, indeed."

Ash watched him program a filter modification on his lab station for a full minute before his implication clicked into place. "I'm not a robot!"

"Yes, that would be the logical conclusion."

She growled in frustration. It had been a long night, and she had only caught Leonard because he was up before the sun to work in the lab. "I'm going after Hector."

The man didn't look up from his screen. "I saw him from the Commons dome as the storm cleared. He stepped willingly into a walker the size of a house."

"He took a spider?"

Leonard looked up at her through his oddly shaped glasses. "It was the kraken variety. I hadn't seen one before, but the hundred tentacles gave it away."

"Will you come with?"

He clicked his tongue. "Too much work to do here, I'm afraid. The reservoir is teeming with new life."

Ash left the lab, exhausted and upset. She wouldn't get any scientists to come to Pyramid. Catastrophes left too many opportunities for innovation, and all the scientists could think of was the expansion of their particular fields of study. Those greedy jerks.

"Maybe she's a cloned supersoldier," said Palak, seated on the front stoop of the tiny home where Ash had sheltered so long ago. "Designed for peak physical perfection."

Ash blinked. "That doesn't explain why she would look like me at all."

Palak's eyes caressed Ash's body in a way that felt more than a little dirty. "Doesn't it?"

All the words drained right out the back of Ash's head.

After taking a deep pull from a flask of strong-smelling nectar, Palak said, "I'll go."

"Thanks," said Ash, leaving as quickly as she could.

Juliette raised an eyebrow. "Well, I didn't see her, but the rumor is that she looks just like you." She wore a net over her hair and smelled like a glitching chemical printer.

"I know that, but why do you think that is?"

Juliette tapped a finger to her lips. "I don't suppose there's enough information to create an informed hypothesis."

Ash sputtered, "That's the worst answer!"

Juliette put a hand on her hip. "It's not wrong."

"Sometimes it's better to be wrong than to have no answer at all."

"Really? Here I was under the impression you were always right."

Sharp words died at the tip of Ash's tongue. She had been around town to her most trusted friends. Almost all of them had sent her away. In the morning, Ash would leave with little backup and no idea if she was doing the right thing.

"Will you come with?" Ash asked, her voice raw with emotion.

"Only if you give me time to pack a full medical support system in that spider."

"Fine."

"And you have to let me drive."

"You know how to drive a walker?"

A wide grin wandered onto Juliette's face. "No, but I think I'd like to learn."

CHAPTER NINE

Ash lingered in the shadows of the Archive, low under the slanted roof in the sparkling hours before dawn. She wore her darkest outfit: a black trench coat, fedora, and matching black gloves. The morning's cold darkness swallowed her, and Simon was late.

"Ash!" he shouted, rounding the building. "Where have you been?"

Ash stepped from her shadow. "I've been recruiting people."

"You were supposed to meet me ten minutes ago."

"I was right here. In the shadows."

Simon shook his head. "First of all, this isn't a heist. You're allowed to just come in."

"Excellent. Elaborate con jobs make the best heists."

"Second, the best place to hide is always in plain sight."

Ash narrowed her eyes. She removed her fedora and placed it on his head. "Lead the way, partner. I need that tablet to find Hector, and I'm not leaving without it."

"You won't find him." Moira stood in the doorway. "You'll only cause more trouble."

Simon held out a hand to stop Ash before she did anything stupid. She pushed it aside and got right up in Moira's face. Moira didn't flinch.

"Tell me what you know, Moira," Ash growled. "Or else."

Moira narrowed her eyes, and a smug smile crossed her lips. "You don't have the patience to be an archivist, my dear. I think you're going to need to be banned again."

"Ash, please. Stop." Simon tried to separate the two women, but Ash shoved him away.

Right in Moira's face, she said, "What do you know?"

Moira searched Ash's face. "You won't like it."

"I already don't like it."

The archivist ushered them into the building and started toward the far set of stairs.

"What about the elevator?" Ash asked.

"We'll walk."

Ash's bones ached from exhaustion. "We're in a hurry."

"No elevators," Moira said.

"But—"

"We have no power," Simon explained. "At least, we don't have enough extra power to run the elevators."

The ache in Ash's brain almost found it funny how the one time she might be allowed to use the elevator it wasn't working due to the nature of the emergency.

The three started down the long flight of stairs, Ash's sore muscles protesting her second go at the staircase in as many days. Had that only been yesterday that she'd dropped off the tablet? The walk down into the depths of the Archives felt longer this time. Darker. There were no other archivists so early in the morning. No hushed discussions behind closing doors. Even the databank computers were silent.

"Is everything down?" Ash asked Simon as they passed another door.

"The storm didn't hit us directly, but it disrupted our power grid. Anything sourced outside the Archive's solar captures is down. Those that work on battery backup are still in good shape."

"I didn't realize it was so bad."

"It's worse," Simon said.

"There's a reason Archivists are sworn to secrecy," Moira said. "There are some things colonists do not need to know."

"I didn't know you were—"

"Because it's a secret."

Ash bristled at this. "Who decides that?"

Moira stopped on the stairs and turned to peer at Ash. "You think our motivations are corrupt, but I assure you our motivation is not the problem."

So, there was a problem. "I just want Hector back."

"That might not be something I can give you." Moira continued her long walk down the stairs. "But I can help you understand your situation."

They reached the steel door at the bottom of the pit. Moira painstakingly unlocked it, and when the door swung open the lights lazily woke. At the center of the room, the tablet sat in the center of the table, right where Ash had left it. Next to it were several gold slates containing translation hieroglyphics.

"I haven't had much of a chance to study it," said Simon. "But it's pretty close to a language I can read."

"Did you find any information on their technologies?" Ash asked. "Anything about atmospheric modification? Why did they take Hector?"

"There are only two local datastores on this device. The first is a map of the colony, complete with the latest report on its functionality."

The screen showed the roster list of the Pyramid colony. Thousands of colonists lived there, and their last known state was in almost all cases listed as "stasis." All but two.

But names and their statuses weren't what drew Ash's attention. It was their pictures.

The first was a white-haired middle-aged woman

with brown eyes that seemed to stare beyond the confines of the image. She was the woman whom Palak had mistaken for Ash, only, without the goggles the likeness was considerably less.

She's not you.

Ash blinked. She referenced the translation sheet and sounded out the label on the image. "I know that name." Adaline Pascal. It sounded so familiar. "She doesn't look anything like me."

"She looks exactly like you," Simon replied. "She even has that wild, kinda crazy look in her eyes that you get when you're going to do something stupid."

"That's not a look that I have."

"It is," Moira said. "Even I recognize it."

"She's older than me," Ash said. "And Simon, you're terrible at recognizing people. You thought Winston was Alexander for six months until you finally saw them in the same place."

"They kept pretending to forget what I told them!"

"Because they were different people." Ash jabbed a finger at the screen. "She's not me."

Moira slid the screen away from Ash and switched to a second image. "This may interest you."

On the screen stood a version of Hector with graying hair and lean muscle instead of all the huggable weight that her Hector carried. He wore a black suit with crisp lines that complemented his muscular frame.

"Push the button that explains why there are

copies of Hector and me in Pyramid," Ash said.

"There's no such button," said Moira. "Nor is there anything in our archives to explain it. This is new."

"Maybe they're from an alternate universe," Ash said.

"The interesting part," Moira said, ignoring the comment, "is this." She pulled up a datasheet on the other Hector and a long stream of text flowed by.

Ash scanned the highlighted text. "I can't read that."

Simon squinted at the text. "Retrieve and reinsert."

Ash stared at the screen for several seconds while the pieces fell into place. "This is old data, taken from the moment we disconnected from Pyramid's system. They have a standing order to retrieve and reinsert Hector into the system, and instead of their Hector they took ours?"

"That story fits," Moira said. "And now that she has him, she has no reason to cause us more trouble."

"But why are there clones!"

Moira pressed her lips together. "We know cloning is possible."

"I had *parents,*" said Ash. "Genetic parents. One of the first things I ever tried when I learned biology was the sequencing of their DNA." Unless—unless Traverse had faked that too. "But why?"

Simon placed his hand on Ash's shoulder. "I'm sorry, Ash."

Without looking up from the screen, Ash said, "I have to go after him."

Moira placed a hand on each of their shoulders. "It's safest for everyone if you leave it be."

"Not for Hector."

Moira sighed. "He made a choice."

"He was coerced!" Ash shouted.

Simon cut in. "Hector decided to sacrifice himself so that the rest of us would be safe. We need to respect that."

"I will never respect anything that puts Hector in danger," Ash seethed. "I'm going to get him back, whether I have your help or not."

For a tense held breath, Ash thought they would send her away to solve the problems on her own. Finally, Moira said, "There is more on the device that you will need. Schematics of Pyramid. It could prove quite useful."

Ash said, "I'm going to need someone to read the tablet."

"Do you know why I was sent down to the planet?" Moira whispered.

Ash faced the white-haired woman. "To be a pain in the ass to people who just want to watch the occasional Earth show or read a romance novel?"

Simon elbowed her.

"What?" Ash shook her head. "You're here to keep us from getting too much information."

Surprisingly, Moira agreed. "I keep you from getting too much information, but also I make sure you have the information you need to do your job. That is our mission here in the Archives."

"Great. So you're just working for the big machine upstairs. Has anyone mentioned to you that we don't exactly trust our robot overlord?"

"A robot overlord would have a body," Moira said.

"Right, and Traverse is all around us. Everywhere we go to do whatever it is we do. It's always watching and always listening."

A mischievous smile crinkled the corners of Moira's eyes. "Except for here."

"And my house," Ash said.

Simon cocked his head. "What?"

"I might have finally broken all the cameras when Traverse wouldn't tell me what happened to Hector," said Ash.

"The ones you found." Moira took a step closer to Ash and whispered, "There are ears everywhere, Ash. In the quarry, in the spiders we use to travel everywhere, and in your house where you think you've found all the listening devices. Traverse is everywhere."

"Except for here."

"Exactly."

Ash glanced down at the tablet. "How does this matter to Hector?"

Moira crossed past Ash and picked up the tablet. She disconnected the cables and handed the device to Ash. "You need this to go after him."

Ash looked down at the device. "I can't read it."

"Don't give the tablet power until you pass the first pylon on the pyramid road. After that point it will connect to their instance of Traverse and Simon can interpret for you."

"Hold on." Simon sputtered.

Ash put an arm around his shoulders. "How will we stop them? The bugs, the woman who looks a little bit but not a lot like me. What do I do?"

Simon pulled away from her. "I can't—"

"You need to convince her that Hector belongs with you." Moira took Ash's hand in her own. "This will be worse than you imagine, Ash. Much worse."

"Moira," Simon said, "what are you saying?"

Moira looked at him as if she just remembered he was there. "Simon, you need to go with her. Take the tablet and help her navigate as best you can. Document everything."

Simon swallowed hard. "Olympia is *not* going to like this."

"You always wanted to go on an adventure," Ash said.

"No," he replied. "I never really did."

"Even a little?"

"Nope."

"Huh." Ash started the long climb up the stairs. "Then why do you keep finding yourself at the center of the colony's worst troubles?"

"I don't know, Ash," Simon said as he started after her. "I just don't know."

CHAPTER TEN

THE HAIL STARTED at the edge of the black desert, as they passed through the first of many pylons. Thousands of black stones dropped from high in the sky. The noise on the outside of the spider sounded like Sky itself might crack in half from the cacophony. Casual conversation became impossible and stepping outside the spider became a death sentence.

Ash pushed forward. It was her turn to drive again, and Simon sat next to her. He powered up the tablet and connected to the Pyramid network. Green light washed over his face as he pored over the scrolling text.

Hours passed. Ash remembered driving this same spider along this same route, not knowing if she would arrive to find Hector dead. Raw waves of anxiety and fear rolled over her, but she blinked back the tears. Fought back the thoughts of failure.

Finally, Ash caught sight of the final sentry

pylon. It glowed a furious blue through the torrent of sandy-filled wind, and a sizzle of power hummed in her bones.

"Switch with me," Ash shouted to Simon. "You drive for a while."

Simon was *not* a good driver. Not like Juliette. It had taken them two days to travel to the edge of the desert. The spider lurched and swayed as each took their turns at controls. Ash's muscles ached and her head was filled with a sleep-deprived fog.

"It says no entry," Simon said, reading the tablet as he handed it to her. "The security perimeter is active."

"Hector's going to be really mad when he sees how badly you ruined the paint on his spider," Ash said as a particularly strong blast of sand raked across their carapace.

The raging cacophony swallowed Simon's next words whole. Ash suspected she didn't want to hear it anyway. Simon brought the walker to a stop in front of the last pylon.

The intercom light flashed and Palak's voice crackled through the noise. "What is going on out there?"

Ash shouted back, "It's the final pylon. Not a big deal!"

"The one that might kill us?" said Palak.

"Maybe."

The winds increased, intensifying the clatter of stones against the spider's carapace.

The tablet's data ports flashed, and Ash found she had access to Pyramid's systems, even though she still couldn't read the language.

"Seriously, what is going on up there?" Palak demanded. "Juliette is getting bored."

"I'm not," said Juliette.

"Ash is trying to do the one thing I came along for," said Simon.

Palak spat her words as if they were bitter. "Tell her to quit meddling."

"Settle down," said Juliette. "They'll figure it out."

Juliette and Palak continued the debate in back, but they were low and Ash couldn't hear them. It didn't matter, because she was busy trying to interpret the tablet options. "What does this say?" she asked.

"Personalization."

"Really?" Ash pushed buttons at random. The screen turned blue. Then green. "Huh."

"Disable the field," said Simon.

"How?"

A particularly large rock hit a leg, lurching their spider to one side. It straightened up, but the ride gained a hitch-sway indicative of a broken leg.

Simon said. "I'm telling Hector you did that."

"The map!" Ash exclaimed. On the screen, the colony map's labels became information hotlinks, and she navigated through them as quickly as she could. The words and symbols were written in the Pyramid language, but she picked out the meaning of a few. In several locations, nodes opened to something that looked like an inventory list.

Of people.

Hundreds of pictures scrolled by, and she almost didn't pay them any heed. Then, one caught her eye.

"Ash, just disable the defensive field."

Orson. The kind barkeep running the Commons. It was him, right there on the Pyramid list. Only, this version of him had a slightly wider nose and a scar above his eye. Ash started paying closer attention, picking up others from the list who looked suspiciously like people she knew from Edge. Del was there, just as grumpy-looking in Pyramid as she had been in Edge. And their version of Leonard had his hair cropped short. It didn't look bad.

Ash stopped herself. She could have scrolled through the inventory all day looking for people similar to those she found in Edge.

"Do you think we're all clones?" Ash's voice shook a little more than she intended.

Silence. Real, true silence. Ash looked up from her screen to see a perfectly still sky.

"The storm stopped," she said.

"It doesn't matter if we're clones," Simon muttered.

Ash narrowed her eyes. "You know something."

He pointed at the tablet. "So could you, if you thought about it. What we need right now is a plan to get Hector back."

"Are you a clone?" Ash asked.

Simon blinked slowly. "In every scientific experiment there are controls and there are variables."

"I bet I'm a variable," said Ash. She totally had to be a variable. That still didn't explain Adaline, though. Unless...

A memory tickled the back of her head. On the screen, she navigated to the central chamber where she and Hector had first seen the sarcophagi. Adaline Pascal's name came up first on the inventory. Ash stared at the woman's face. "I remember her."

Simon looked at her as if she were stupid, even though she definitely wasn't.

"Fine," Ash said. She switched the map's view to the central pyramid, where the Commons would have been on a map of Edge. It was the most prominent building, so it was as good a place as any to start.

"It's a fusion plant," Ash said. She poked at the screen. "See here? Air intake on the sides of the pyramid focus in on the central section. Fusion happens here in the middle and exhaust vents up through the top in the form of..." She couldn't continue. The implications astounded her. "Why didn't Victor want us to go in there?"

"Why did he want anything?" Simon asked. "I've never trusted that guy."

"Can we get in by going under like we did before?"

Simon reached over and adjusted the screen. "It

doesn't connect. You were never really in the pyramid."

"Ha!" Ash pumped her fist. "One rule we didn't break."

She peered at the adjusted view of the screen. The display showed the inputs and outputs of the fusion plant in the center of the pyramid. Everything they needed was here. The excess and increasing oxygen, the persistent sediment in the air. All of it originated with this lone machine. How long had it been running?

"What?" Simon asked. "What is it?"

"We need to shut down that power plant."

Simon furrowed his brow. "How does that help Hector?"

Ash turned back to her tablet to find an indicator blinking in the corner. "What's going on?"

Simon peered at the message on the screen and scrunched up his nose. "You're getting an incoming call."

"Who is it?"

"Do you have a lot of friends here?"

"Not yet." Ash pressed the button and a face appeared on the screen.

Her doppelgänger, Adaline Pascal stared back at her through hazy goggles. "You followed me," the woman said with a sharp accent.

"You have someone that belongs to me," said Ash.

The other woman said, "Why do you look like me?"

Ash bristled at the formal tone of the other woman's voice, but it still rang true to her memory. "My name's Ash," Ash said. "How do I know you're not Traverse pretending to be Adaline Pascal, hoping to manipulate me into leaving you alone."

On the screen, Adaline's lips pressed into a tight line. "So you know about that."

"I know about a lot of things," Ash said. "Shut down the pyramid and give us back Hector. Then we'll leave."

This time Adaline frowned. "Shutting down this facility would be suicide for me and my people."

"Your pyramid is killing this planet."

"You're a danger to us all," said Adaline. A frustrated scowl flashed across her face.

"Maybe," Ash said, "but I have information you want. Drop the barrier, call off those bugs, and let us walk right in the front door."

The sky darkened. Wind picked up again, battering sand against the spider in a long, low hiss.

"What do you know?" Adaline said.

"If I tell you that, then you won't let us in."

"If you tell me, I won't need to kill you."

Wind swirled around the spider. Ash cast a nervous glance at Simon, but he didn't move.

"We're fine," Ash told him. "Everything's perfectly fine."

"Tell me what you know," Adaline said again. In the final pylon, a crackle of energy popped, and the field went still.

Simon walked their spider through and right up against the wall where sand piled much higher than last time. The outside gate, still slightly ajar, now sat half-buried in black sand. He set the spider down outside the door. The plan had been to push the door farther open and park inside, but they wouldn't be able to do that now that the gate was buried under a drift.

"Life was good in the borough," said Ash to the screen. "My parents took care of me. The other children studied hard, too, but I was always the best in math and science."

The spider shook as the wind whipped faster. A blast of sand struck the side of the machine. It piled up against the cockpit window and its fury thrummed in Ash's bones.

"When I was little, my world was pretty small. I interacted with a couple dozen people—tops—so when someone new came into my life, I noticed."

Ash gazed at the screen. That one memory, lingering deep in her past struggled to match up with the image she had seen on the tablet. To a child, every adult was ancient. The woman was too cruel, but maybe Ash's innocence of youth had softened Adaline Pascal in her mind.

"I noticed, and I remember it, even though I was very little," Ash said. "I remember the one day my mother introduced me to someone I had never met before."

Adaline watched in silence as Ash wiped away tears.

"I'm your granddaughter," Ash finally said. "Adaline Pascal, you are my grandmother on my mother's side."

The memories of children were faulty things. Ash might have been completely wrong about everything. This Adaline might have been a clone, because apparently that was something she needed to worry about now. Ash's admission was a gamble.

The wind died, and Ash's ears rang with the void of silence left behind. For a long time, Adaline peered at Ash through the tablet screen.

"The granddaughter," Adaline finally said. "I remember you. Kamala finally did something right, then, didn't she?"

CHAPTER ELEVEN

Ash shone against the glistening black sand, her all-white gear wrapped around her like armor against the forbidden land. She stretched her stiff joints under reinforced padding. The printers in Edge wouldn't print armor, but they would print gear designed to withstand a variety of harsh conditions. If she had to go against a swarm of robotic locusts, she wanted protection. Her white cloak draped off her shoulders, and she wore white-rimmed goggles to protect her eyes and face, because if she had to walk into a hostile city, she was definitely going to do it with style.

Palak wore padding under layers of ragged black cloth. She clutched a long metal spear in one hand. Sand crunched under her heavy boots.

Simon and Juliette fastened their gear in the spider. He wore a long red coat and Ash's fedora. She wore reinforced padding under loose coveralls.

Ash touched the knife at her side, assuring herself

of its comforting presence. This was one of Hector's knives, forged rather than printed so that it might better keep its razor-sharp edge.

"You have to see this." Palak crouched in the corner of the entryway courtyard, where the swirling wind had deposited dozens of nutrient brick containers.

Ash poked one with her toe. "Empty."

Palak nodded.

"Seth?" Ash asked, but then where was Seth's spider? Why would he leave garbage here?

Palak looked like she wanted to say more, but instead, she clutched her spear and pressed her lips closed. There were more than a few days' worth of wrappers littering the entryway.

Simon squeezed through the gate. He held the Pyramid tablet and navigated through the linked text.

"Is the signal working?" he asked, touching the comm unit clipped to his shoulder.

"I see the map and some squiggly lines," Juliette said through the comm. She sat safely behind the controls of the spider.

"Good," said Ash. "See if you can excavate that door and wait for my signal."

Simon tossed a small backpack to Ash. "You're supposed to carry this around until you have your pack mule back, whatever that means."

"Thanks." Ash slung the pack over her shoulder.

With a clunk and a long moan, the inner gate

opened on its own to reveal a gaping hole into writhing darkness.

"Well, that's somewhat ominous," Ash muttered.

Simon swallowed hard.

"Didn't that open onto the streets last time?" Palak said. She gripped her spear loosely at her side and stepped in front of the others.

Ash touched her on the arm. "I'll go first."

Palak nodded. A tunnel of twisting tentacles arched over the street like black ribs. They swayed like weeds deep below the sea. Ash stepped across the threshold, with Simon and Palak trailing close.

Adaline stood, dressed all in black, with goggles pushed back against a mass of tangled hair.

"Granddaughter," the woman rasped.

"Grandmother." Seeing the woman now, the creases on her face, and the severity in her eyes, Ash finally, completely believed that this was the woman she'd met so long ago. She hadn't aged at all, but it was her.

The two women stood facing each other, one in white, the other in black. Up close, Ash spotted golden nodes in Adaline's scalp under that matted hair, similar to the nodes embedded in Victor's skull. Neurological links, as far as Ash could gather. Control nodes for the nearby defenses, most likely. This close, Ash could also see the differences between herself and the older woman. Their eyes had a different shape, and the wrinkles at the corners of Adaline's mouth hinted at a frown.

"I see the difference now," said Simon. "She's taller."

Ash stretched her back, hoping better posture might make up the difference. It didn't.

Adaline gestured for them to follow through the long tunnel. "Your mother only introduced me to you once."

"You only visited that once."

"I remember a curious little girl." Adaline waved with two fingers and the tentacles parted, creating a path that took them deeper into the city. "Time has been harsh. It always is, isn't it?"

"You killed our guinea pigs and poisoned our lake."

Disgust twisted the corner of Adaline's mouth. "We rid you of a pest and seeded your lake with a thousand species. Your water will thrive for a thousand years because of my gift."

"Your attack killed people."

Adaline's gloved hands constricted into claws. "Sometimes great deeds require sacrifice."

"We don't trade human lives."

"The steward comes willingly, and I have seen your colony. It lacks advances in science and technology that would raise it to greatness." She gestured with her hands and the tentacles parted to reveal a view of the pyramid. Lines along its black surface glowed with a deep violet in the dark hour before morning.

"We don't need greatness," Ash said without a single ounce of conviction.

Adaline continued down the tentacle-shrouded road. "Come, I will let you discuss this with your friend. He is being quite stubborn."

The tentacles parted and the sky opened before them. Ash peered up through the crystalline night. Something sparkled in the wind, reflecting a violet glow emanating from the pinnacle of the central pyramid. It was the sediment that graced all the air on Sky, but here the concentration was enough to choke the filter of her rebreather and form a crust in the creases of her skin.

They passed the biolab, where Ash and Hector had found an entrance to the Pyramid tombs. The walls no longer showed damage, and clusters of tentacles repaired the remaining marks in the area. They secreted a pungent slurry, which hardened when struck with a powerful beam of light. Using this, the writhing masses printed ornate patterns on otherwise drab surfaces, as if doodling in the corners of a notebook.

"It's beautiful," Ash said.

Simon stepped up beside her. "It's creepy."

"I failed to convince your mother to do something useful," said Adaline. "She insisted on staying to help breeders aboard the ship when all of the tests showed she had a mind for real science."

"She did pretty well for herself."

Adaline's accent intensified. "Not that breeders

aren't important for the sake of the colony. Quite important, really."

"She didn't tell me much about you," Ash said. "Only that you died. I almost didn't remember your name."

"Being exiled to the surface is a kind of death, granddaughter. This world is the afterlife that reflects our sins above."

"So, a tentacle-world filled with stinging death bugs is your afterlife? I think I'd like to know more about how you lived to earn that."

"Only the strongest deserve life here," Adaline said.

"What happens to the weak?"

Adaline stopped. The tentacles nearest her twitched in irritation. "What happened to your mother?"

"Retirement."

The older woman's shoulder sagged. "I am sorry to hear it." Adaline's rolling accent clouded her words.

"How long were you in stasis?" Ash asked.

"Years do not matter here—only progress. The world changes slowly, and our most brilliant scientists built a way for us to be around when their work was complete."

"Some say that progress matters, but people matter more." Ash swallowed. "And freedom. For those people. Like Hector, for instance."

"That's a great saying," whispered Palak. "I hear that one all the time."

Adaline cocked her head. "The steward cannot leave. This colony will die without him." When Ash didn't respond, she continued, "Very few of us have the ability to reenter stasis once we are out, so there are a number of safeguards to keep us from coming out. My stasis allows for an override if I wish to wake."

"Like if someone comes poking around your ruins."

"It woke me once when the last steward died. Then, it woke me again when the new steward approached. Nobody else in the colony will wake unless your friend specifically wakes them."

"That makes no sense at all."

"They will stay in stasis forever until the machines fail and they die."

"So, let's wake them all up."

"The world is not yet prepared for them."

"What are they waiting for? Prairies and forests? Wake them up."

Adaline gestured at the city. "A death sentence, to wake them all right now. There are no resources. It will be a thousand years before our paradise is complete."

Ash grabbed Adaline's arm and pulled her around to face her. "Where are you taking us?"

Adaline spread her palms to show them where they

were. They had entered a wide alcove at the base of the pyramid, and the tentacles shading their road opened like petals of a flower. The night sky sparkled above, and the pyramid loomed like a giant above them. In the center of the alcove sat a dry fountain covered in twisted statues. At the base of the statues, in the center of a twisted mass of stone, stood a matte-black monolith.

"What is this place?" Simon asked, then, staring at his tablet, answered his own question. "Oh, this taps directly into the network."

"There are few enough of these remaining." Adaline touched the side of the monolith, and it split open with a great sigh. "This is how you may speak with the steward."

Palak backed away. "This isn't good, Ash."

"Yeah, I can see that." But could she? If this was how she could talk to Hector, then this was how she could find Hector. Was he in stasis already? "Maybe if I just go in a little bit."

Palak clutched her spear. "Take us to Hector," she said to Adaline. "Now."

Simon closed the tablet and held it close. "I don't like this."

Juliette, over the comm, said, "Ash?"

Ash ignored the call. She had to think.

Adaline watched them with an amused expression. She said, "Nobody dies here, granddaughter. We live effectively forever in stasis, as the world is made perfect for our return. From time to time a few of us wake to walk in the world and make adjustments."

"But you're killing this world," Ash said. "Your paradise will never happen."

"I'm offering you a chance to speak with the steward in our afterlife, but death—there is no death."

Palak lowered her spear at Adaline. "No death? Would you like to tell my brother about how there's no death?"

"Ash?" Juliette said over the comm. "Simon, what is going on?"

"Ash is going to make bad decisions again," Simon whispered back to her.

"Tell me about the destruction in the lab?" Ash asked of her grandmother. "Something exploded there. When Hector and I came to visit, we saw bodies. There's ruin all over this city, and something wrong with the power plant."

"Sabotage," said Adaline. "From long ago."

Juliette said, "I found Seth's spider buried in sand."

The telltale hum of an energy weapon called out into the night air. Its low pitch made the hair on the back of Ash's neck stand up. She knew that sound. "Seth," she shouted, "you might as well come out."

"Thought you folk might be able to lure the lady out," Seth said, stepping around a cluster of disabled tentacles. He leveled the long weapon at Adaline. "I think it's about time we talk a little more about this 'no death' thing."

"Put it down, Seth," Ash said. "She's going to let me talk to Hector. We'll get this figured out."

He took a step forward. "I think I'd rather hear some answers straight from her." To Adaline, he said, "You know what I'm here for."

Adaline's expression darkened. "Who sent you?" The tentacles around her went dead still.

"Said it's called a scarab." Seth gestured at the pyramid with his gun. "I figure there's one up in there since I haven't found one down here in the city."

"That's what got Harish killed?" Ash asked. "You entered the pyramid, didn't you?"

Seth spat. "I told him to head back. He followed and messed it all up."

Palak snarled, "You!" She swung her spear to face him.

Seth trained the gun on her and clicked his tongue. "I think you know how this fight ends up."

The tentacles behind Adaline rippled. "None but the steward may enter the pyramid." To Ash, she said, "This is an antiquated access port, meant for temporary insertion. It will let you visit the steward, but only through this." She gestured at the black monolith.

"Why do you call him that?" Ash asked.

Adaline pressed her lips together.

"Ash," Palak rasped without taking her eyes off Seth.

Ash took a step toward the maw. "I think I have to do this."

"You're just going to trust her?" Simon said.

"What choice do I have?"

Adaline said, "It won't put you in stasis and it can't sustain you forever. Time to speak with the steward. That is all."

Seth's muscles quivered with tension. "I want my answers."

Ash said, "I think—"

"No!" he shouted. "I'm in charge this time. We're not doing one damn thing this woman wants. It's a trick and we're not falling for it. Harish went into one of those things."

"Very well." Adaline reached up very slowly, pulled her goggles down over her eyes, and brushed the dust from the front of her black outfit. "This is not how I wanted this to go."

And the tentacles struck. They hit Seth's weapon first, smacking the barrel hard. A searing hot bolt struck the writhing mess behind Palak. Tentacles twisted around Seth's right arm. Then his leg. He struggled against it. Twisted.

Simon stumbled backward, tablet in his hands.

Palak pounced at Adaline, lunging with the spear, but a tentacle snatched her out of the air. It dragged her away, and more tentacles closed around her.

Ash was frozen. Unable to decide in the furious chaos around her. What if she chose wrong?

Seth, with a shout of rage, wrenched the still-charging energy weapon to bear and fired a bolt at Adaline.

The world shifted. Tentacles swelled in place to block the attack, partially deflecting the splash of energy. Adaline screamed as tentacles melted and her flesh sizzled. The black sleeve on her right arm melted and peeled away.

She scrambled, fear flashing behind the glass of her goggles.

"Seth, stop!" Ash cried. She stepped between the man and Adaline.

For a moment that stretched into an aching eternity, Seth didn't move. The tentacles holding him dropped uselessly to his sides, disabled by some unseen force. As he lowered his weapon, a grin spread over his face. "You don't understand, Ash."

A tentacle slammed into Seth from the side. He flew, tumbling hard on the pavement. The weapon skittered away.

And landed across the courtyard at Palak's feet. She picked up the weapon.

"You have some explaining to do," she said to Seth. She pointed the gun at Seth. "And I think you know how this fight goes."

A dark figure loomed behind her, fists full of tentacles torn from the walls.

Harish. Alive.

The man's face was gaunt, and his eyes were full of cold rage that sent a chill down Ash's spine. His mole stood out as a black dot against his pale skin.

Slowly, Seth stood and brushed himself off. "I can explain." He made a gesture and the tentacles around him dropped away. "Victor taught me a few tricks."

Palak leveled the weapon at Seth.

A flash of cruel rage flashed over Adaline's face. "Victor," she spat. "*He* sent you?"

Her upper lip twitched, and a hundred tentacles burst forward, forming a wall that blocked Seth, Palak, and Harish from Ash and Adaline.

"Speak with the steward," Adaline rasped. "Now." She gestured with an open palm, and tentacles launched at Ash.

She dodged one, only to have the other two grasp both of her arms. "This isn't helping me trust you," she said.

Adaline strolled forward. "I should have known that heretic still lived. I should have guessed that he would send you to destroy us."

The tentacles pulled Ash further back. She struggled, but it was like pulling against steel cable. "It's not like that," she said. Wasn't it? Victor *had* sent them. Why?

Behind the newly formed wall, the energy weapon fired. Then again, but farther away. Harish's roar of rage echoed throughout the city.

Ash was only steps away from the gaping maw. It wasn't black inside like she previously thought. It was a million glittering pins. Tiny tentacles reached for her.

Simon stepped from the shadows next to the machine. He punched at the tablet controls. "I think I'm figuring this out," he said, pressing forward. "There's just so much of it."

The tentacles on Ash's arms loosened, and she wriggled free.

Adaline watched, a coolly impassive expression on her face. "I can do this without you, but this is your last chance to see our steward."

The weapon fired again, this time even farther away. Ash drew a breath. She couldn't afford to worry about them. Harish was alive. Alive! Their previous mission had been a failure, but at least nobody had died. A fresh wave of confidence surged at the thought that maybe, just maybe, she could trust her instinct on this. She glanced at the dark maw.

Glowing pinpricks of light glittered in the dark. The space within held tech like none she'd ever seen.

If Adaline wasn't lying, it was her chance to see Hector.

"Simon," she said, forcing her voice to calm down. "I'm going in."

He mashed at the tablet controls. "I don't know what it will do."

"I need to find out."

Simon looked up at her. The energy weapon fired again, and a wave of heat washed over them.

"You're trusting your grandmother?" Simon said. "Really?"

Ash spread her arms wide and stepped into the

open machine. "Have a little faith, Simon." She turned to meet his gaze as she sunk into the glittering black. "You remember what our goals here are, right?" she whispered, glancing at Adaline.

Simon nodded.

"Good. Then run."

The machine swallowed her, and the whole world fell up and away into the sky.

CHAPTER TWELVE

In the beginning, there was nothing.

A million microscopic tendrils wormed over her flesh, touched her eyes and ears, and coiled around her fingers. Gold, glowing hairs streamed into her body, overwhelming every sense. They held her so tight she could not breathe. The world constricted to a single point.

Then, there was everything.

Pyramid surrounded her and assaulted her senses. She almost *was* Pyramid, flexing muscles woven of organic metals. Breathing through the conduits of power and information. Streets and buildings became extensions of her limbs.

Too much. Too much!

Nothing, again. Only the rapid, irregular beat of her heart. Ash flexed inside the system, bringing segments online with careful meditations upon the individual inputs. Flex and release. Muscles. Fractals of movement and direction. She saw through strange eyes, experiencing the world in an ever-changing three-dimensional space.

Seth wandered the dark underbelly of her city. He passed glowing blue sarcophagi containing the living remains of a thousand colonists. Ash sensed the potential of their unbeating hearts. Each was a frozen knot of flame ready to burst forth.

"Harish, stop!" called Palak. She rushed after her brother in the blasted-out ruins elsewhere in the city. Below them, the catacombs lay open, bare to the unceasing sky. Tentacles dared not approach this ruined junction that they'd failed to rebuild so many times before. There was something wrong here. A malevolent will controlled the power junction, and it drew so much power.

Power. A fusion reaction hummed in her bones. She felt it as it roared in the night. It felt wrong. Inefficient. Old. It produced oxygen as its output, but also the fine dust that formed the desert around them. The pyramid was the source. Why hadn't Victor wanted her to go there—to see that central structure?

Traverse's influence still lingered, but Pyramid still existed in the AI's aftermath, destroyed by its own willful independence.

Harish pulled up to a stop before the pyramid. His hands gripped the weapon as if it might save him. He said, "I thought I would die here."

Palak placed a hand on one of her brother's big arms. "Seth said—"

"We climbed in through the vents halfway up when they opened in the morning. Seth said he knew where the scarab was."

"What scarab?" Palak asked.

"I don't know what it was. He knew where he was going, but when he opened the central chamber, he released the bugs." Harish held out his hands, showing a dozen shallow cuts along his arms. "Seth pushed me and I fell back into the swarm. I think he meant it as a distraction so that he could escape."

"He pushed you?"

Confusion slipped across Harish's face. Ash's view flickered and refocused on a dark space in a different part of Pyramid.

"Ash," said Simon. "Can you hear me?"

Simon hid in a cramped closet. Above, a knot of tentacles draped useless from the ceiling.

"Simon," Ash said. She heard her own voice, and it took a moment to realize she spoke through the tablet that he still carried.

"I thought that might work." Simon continued to speak, but his voice echoed into the distance. "It's like a plea for your attention. You exist in the space Traverse occupies in Edge." Then he flickered, and Ash was swept away again.

She stood in a white void. Next to her, stood Adaline.

The void parted like dense fog to reveal a pristine Pyramid settlement, devoid of the ravages of time and the destruction of the furious winds. People populated the streets, and they wore fashions Ash had never seen. Robes cut for equal parts flowing style and luxurious comfort. Colors that her printers had trouble producing, like the green of sunset or the rich blue of a summer afternoon. They were a grim people, and none of them wore rebreathers.

Adaline spoke in a low voice. "Long ago, our people came to a conclusion. We could survive the world that we had started to build, but we could not thrive. The biggest problems of the rocky planet had been solved. Oxygen filled the air, and the soil around our home grew rich with the humus of our crops. Our fusion plant created enough power to forge this world into the utopia we desired, but it would take time. Too much time."

"So you created the stasis chambers," Ash said.

"There were many solutions proposed. The only one that made sense—that created the world we wanted but also allowed us to live in it—was stasis. Locusts delivered the preparatory nanomachines. The steward's chamber performed the necessary neurosurgery. We could sleep for thousands of years if necessary."

Ash's vision switched. Far away, she saw Harish and Seth fighting atop a narrow bridge between two buildings. The energy weapon was nowhere to be seen, but Harish swung a knife and Seth carried Palak's spear.

Blood gushed from Harish's nose and clogged his rebreather, so he tore it from his face. He held one hand on his ribs. "You knew," he said with a rasping voice between short gasps. "All along."

"I did what I had to do," Seth said. "Nothin' more than that."

Simon's voice echoed in Ash's ears, as if from a great distance. "And if we do that, I think we can shut down their fusion generator, stop oxygen overproduction, and save Hector."

"That's great, let's do it," Ash replied reflexively.

Simon nodded once, packed his things, and ventured back out into the maze of the city.

Palak crept along the lower corridors, somewhere that Ash could barely see. There were places in the city that were not connected to her network, and whole districts she could not influence.

Ash tamped down the overwhelming flow of images. Too much came in all at once, and her head throbbed from the rapid switching.

Adaline continued as if Ash's mind hadn't wandered, "Stasis was the least offensive solution to our problem, but there were others. They risked upsetting the balance we hoped to one day maintain, and worse, they risked upsetting our god. The difficult part was the problem of maintaining our city while we slept."

"What other options were you talking about?"

"None you need to concern yourself with."

"How old is Victor?"

In the vision that followed, the thin, muscle-bound version of Hector stepped to a terminal in the center of a large chamber. He placed a hand on the glass surface and a shimmering blue light bathed him.

"We named a steward to take the place of Traverse, whose duty was to live in the city and keep it pristine until we woke."

"You got rid of Traverse?"

"We limited the machine god, giving it power only where necessary. Little did we know that the heretic did not go into stasis. He continued his research and built machines that angered our god. When he was discovered, what remained of Traverse struck out in the only ways it could."

In the vision, an explosion ripped through the chamber, shredding stasis chambers and injuring a man. In its aftermath, Ash recognized the room.

"This is the lab."

"The heretic's lab was always unstable." Adaline's voice was full of spite. "There should never have been volatile material there."

"Yeah, that's super irresponsible," Ash said.

"Without the steward, the entire colony was doomed. The systems were genetically keyed to him —a precaution we took because of ambitious men like your Victor." In the vision, the city grew old. Edges wore away, and dust piled and blew through empty streets. "When, much later, your mother woke, she knew she had to return to the ship to create a new steward."

"And when you woke you thought you'd check up on her."

"I came to bring her home." Adaline's expression went dark. "But she had you."

Ash's vision flickered. Across the city, Juliette fought a swarm of locusts, crushing them with a wide section of pipe as they swarmed her. She pressed her back against the spider, fighting furiously to keep the insects at bay. The swarm poured over the wall. Palak now chased Seth across the rooftops, firing wildly from the energy weapon. From a distance, Harish followed with a grimace on his pale, bloodied face. He gripped his ribs and limped forward.

"Simon," Ash said.

Simon pulled to a halt in a darkened alley. He pressed up against the base of the pyramid, a sealed entrance only a dozen yards away. "What?"

"Palak, Harish, and Seth are coming your way. Victor said to stay clear of the pyramid, but that's where you need to take them. Hector's in there."

"But the plan—"

"I was paying attention, but—"

"Why would you say that if you were actually paying attention?"

"This is why you always beat me in chess," Ash said.

"You *only* use your queen."

"She's the most badass piece!"

"What does it matter anyway? You cheated your way out of our bet."

"That dress had guinea pig pee on it." It did. "It wasn't my fault." It definitely was.

Simon threw up his hands. "You know what, let's talk chess strategy some other—"

A bolt of raw heat splashed against the wall next to him. Simon dove to the side with a yelp as Seth ran past. He took cover in the alcove of the pyramid entrance.

"Stop!" Ash yelled. "All of you!" The city shook with her voice. "There's a swarm coming."

Simon scrambled to his feet in time to step in front of Palak. He restrained her, but just barely. The gun smoked in her hands.

Palak lowered the weapon. "That asshole tried to kill my brother," she said.

"Deal with that later," said Simon.

"Later?" Palak shoved him away. "How about now?"

Simon raised his hands, palms outward. "We need to get through that door as fast as we can."

A short distance away, Seth said, "Harish tried to kill *me*. I just defended myself." The door next to him opened.

Palak's pushed past Simon, raised her weapon, and fired.

Seth dove into the pyramid.

"No!" Palak yelled. She ran forward and dove through just before the stone slammed shut.

Simon swore.

Then, the swarm hit.

"Call off the bugs," Ash said to Adaline. "Now."

"Give me my steward."

"They're going to kill my friends."

Adaline nodded. "He cannot control them until he joins the machine. He has this choice."

Ash's heart slammed in her chest. She knew the choice Adaline talked about, and it was the worst kind of choice.

It was Hector's choice.

"You said I could speak with him," Ash pleaded. "Where is he?"

A light bloomed to Ash's right, and when she turned she saw another avenue of information open before her. A single step forward, and she stood in a stone room surrounded by the swirling art she'd seen on the buildings outside. Hector huddled in the corner of the room.

Ash's choked on the lump in her throat. "Hey."

Hector looked up. He blinked rapidly. "Ash?"

A holographic projection of her formed before him. She wanted nothing more than to reach out and touch him, but she knew it wasn't possible.

"Hector, I—"

"I know I should have said something before I left," Hector said. "Everything happened so fast. I had to save those people."

Anger bubbled up in Ash's chest. "You went willingly. All you wrote was that she wasn't me."

"She's not."

"That doesn't mean it's a useful thing to say!" Ash shouted.

"I wanted you to follow me."

"I would have no matter what you said."

"She controls everything, Ash. I thought she'd give me time to say goodbye, but there was nothing I could do."

"But you left."

"I'm sorry." He hung his head like a scolded puppy. "And now I don't know what to do."

"You can leave. We'll get you out."

He winced. "This is the last step, and if I go in that machine, I don't know if I'll ever be able to come out, so there's something I want to give you."

Ash reached out as if to take him into her arms before remembering that she was only a hologram here. "If you go in there, I think you can call off the locusts. You can save us."

"Then I have to go in."

"No, you don't." Ash looked around the room again. "This is a decision, Hector. You don't have to do this. We can get you out of there. We can go home. Together."

He took a step toward the gaping sarcophagus. "I don't think you can. There isn't a choice here, Ash. If I go in, I can save everyone. If I don't, we're all going to die."

"It'll change you," Ash said. "It'll hook a machine up to your brain."

He swallowed. "I know." Ash had never seen him really afraid before. He was terrified.

"Adaline—she's my grandmother."

His voice caught. "I didn't know that. It makes

sense. She told me I'm a clone, same as their steward. There were a lot of us a long time ago. Pyramid was supposed to get more, but then something happened with Traverse. We're just workers. Did you know that? We're workers and we're designed to be good at working. Nothing else."

Ash's palms went cold. "You're not a pawn," she said.

"Yeah, I am. I don't know if I'm your pawn or hers, but the choice looks pretty clear. I need to go into the machine, stop the swarm, and then help Adaline manage this whole settlement until it's ready to wake up."

"But she won't ever let you go."

He swallowed hard. "Maybe she will."

Ash whispered, "She's not me."

"It's what it is, Ash. Think about it. Can I really let you die? Can I let the residents of this colony all fade away to nothing? If I take over steward duties here, maybe I can fix the broken fusion reactor. That's what's poisoning the air, isn't it? Adaline explained that the plant is stuck in high gear because of that one broken junction."

"It's not a broken junction. It's Traverse exerting influence. Slowly killing the colony."

He nodded. "Even more important that I do something then."

Ash couldn't stop him. Couldn't move him. Nothing she did could make him step aside.

And then, Hector sang. He was quiet at first, and

his only accompaniment was the echo off the hard stone of the chamber, but as he sang, the song grew. He sang a song for her from old Earth—one from the ancient earthlings who wrote so many powerful songs about love.

It was a song about love, but also a song about saying goodbye. The gift given to her as she left would be his song, and it hurt so much thinking of him turning away from her. He sang, and tears rolled down his face. Ash wanted so much to take hold of him. Gather him up in her arms and never let him go.

But that wasn't to be. She was only a hologram watching him from inside a machine. He was only a man with a broken heart who had gifted her with one last song before stepping into his unknown fate.

When he finished, she whispered, "Elton John?"

"One of the classics," Hector said, wiping away the tears. "I thought you might like it."

"I didn't even know you sang."

"I've been taking lessons from Orson."

She said, "If you really need to be a pawn, then be a pawn. Follow orders and do what your queen tells you to do."

"The queen is the most badass piece, I hear."

"Yeah, well, you hear a lot of things."

Hector closed his eyes and drew in a long, slow breath. "I love you," he said.

"I love you, too, Hector."

With that, Hector stepped into the maw of the machine sarcophagus, and the golden arms of the machine surrounded him, engulfed him, closed him away until there was nothing left.

Ash's data link crashed. Her stomach wrenched and her brain exploded in pain. The city fell away from her, and every nerve in her body screamed a razor's edge of pain. She fell from her machine in a heap and gasped for breath.

A shadow passed over her as Adaline stepped between Ash and the seven moons.

"I want him back," Ash said when she could finally speak. She clawed her fingers into the sandy earth as if feeling something solid might bring her back to reality. It didn't work.

Locusts swarmed around Adaline in a dense cloud. "If he abandons the city, thousands will die."

Ash's head pounded. Breath came in shallow gasps. There had to be a better solution, but her mind couldn't grasp the pieces. "You can't keep him," she said. "I won't let you."

"I know," said Adaline. With a flash of blue, a glowing knife appeared in her hand. "But you've done your part."

CHAPTER THIRTEEN

Ash THREW sand because queens do whatever they want. That's what makes them badass. That's how they win.

Only, she didn't win because Adaline wore goggles and a thin-lipped expression of grim determination. Ash could throw sand at that face all day without causing so much as a distraction. She drew her knife as she stood. It felt clumsy in her hand compared to the twelve-inch glowing blue fire Adaline wielded.

This thought was reinforced when Adaline, as if effortlessly halving a blade of grass, sliced Ash's steel knife in half. Ash retreated.

Adaline pressed forward. "This is nothing personal, dear. Now that the steward is in place, you are a threat to the colony."

Ash threw her knife handle at Adeline's face,

which had almost as much effect as the sand. "Hector's not your steward. He's mine."

"Oh, really?"

The cloud of locusts around Adaline parted, and a knot of them swarmed Ash. They landed on her back and legs, tangling in her white cape with tiny claws. Her armor held, but she felt their razors rasping across reinforced fabric. She resisted the urge to swat them away, seeing it for the distraction it was. A queen had to be clever.

Adaline advanced with measured steps, and Ash scrambled away. She vaulted behind the machine so that there was at least something between the two of them. Her grandmother didn't slow but changed path to circle around the barrier. Blue fire popped and sizzled on her knife.

"It hurts me to do this, dear," said Adaline. "But here in our colony, we've always had high aspirations. And the loftier the goals, the deeper the sacrifice."

Ash backed toward the courtyard exit. If she could squeeze through the gap in tentacles without getting snagged, she might flee. "Is that what I am to you? A sacrifice?"

"Your mother never knew her worth to us. Her skills could have helped us make a hundred stewards. A thousand if needed."

"She was a midwife." A few more steps. Tentacles thrashed as if in a seizure. "She helped deliver babies. She was a pillar of our community."

"A midwife and a breeder. Wasted work for the greatest geneticist this world has ever known."

"I'm not so bad at genetics either, you know."

A thin smile crossed Adaline's lips. "You won't save yourself by appearing to be useful, my dear. With the heretic's technology, all we need is one steward."

"Immortality," Ash said.

"Something like it. The scarab preserves life. Not forever, but for a very long time. You see why this would disrupt the natural order."

Adaline tore her gaze from Ash and focused on the wall of tentacles surrounding the room. Her brow furrowed with concentration.

Yet, the tentacles did nothing.

"Problem?" Ash said. She held her hands palm up, allowing the vicious locusts to land on them. "Hector, if you really have control of these, I could use some help."

They bit and scratched at the cloth of her gloves.

"Damn." She crushed the locust.

Ash remembered the layout of the area. She'd seen it all when she was in the machine. The path Seth and Harish had taken was behind her, an open path for her to cross the whole city. But what would that gain? Could she outrun Adaline?

Did she need to?

Ash ran.

Tentacles rose before her, thrashing at the predawn sky. The buzz of locusts intensified, agitated by her movement. She shouldered through a waving sea of hapless thrashers and mounted a steep slope to land atop a nearby roof. Adaline followed, slashing ropey tentacles with her blue knife. It cut through them like wind, opening a path.

The gap came, where Seth and Harish had fought, then the bridge. Ash jumped where she needed and turned to face Adaline.

Far below, movement caught her eye, and she hoped Adaline didn't notice the red of Simon's jacket as he passed underneath. The plan. What had been Simon's plan? Ash looked to the pyramid, where the light at its top blended with the burning fire of the impending sunrise. They needed to shut off the fusion reactor, free Hector, drop the perimeter defenses, and escape. Simple.

Adaline stepped onto the narrow bridge high above the streets.

Ash had to hold her attention so Simon could pass undetected. "I thought this colony would have useful tech for us, but you have nothing. It's all garbage."

The older woman tensed. She clearly didn't want to step out onto the bridge, where Ash might have a chance to knock her down. "I've seen your backwards colony. You live in poverty, barely feeding your children."

"What do you mean? There were plenty of guinea pigs for everyone."

Adaline took a step forward. "You writhe around

in the vermin and mud, hoping to change the world without any clue what is already in it."

Ash gestured at the city below. "We didn't know the world was poisoned by cancers like Pyramid."

"You have no idea what was here before we came."

Adaline charged across the bridge. Again, Ash ran. She leaped up off the roof, landing on the next building. Locust swarms thinned, but she still had to swat one away before it found the soft skin exposed between her goggles and her rebreather.

Ash ran to the next ledge and jumped. She couldn't keep this up long, but she knew the path she needed to take. Trust in her friends kept her going.

Having bought a few seconds of breathing time, she fished her comm unit from her pocket and fixed it to her shoulder. "Hey, who's on?"

"Damn, finally," said Simon. "I wasn't sure you'd make it."

"Hold that thought."

"What are you doing?" Simon asked.

"Crossing the board as fast as I can."

"This isn't chess."

"It's a queen's gambit."

"You don't even know what that means!"

Ash ran across another roof and jumped as far as she could. This one was the farthest leap yet, and she barely landed on the next building. Behind her, Adaline stood on the roof's edge, unable or unwilling to make the jump.

"Not looking so great now, is it, grandma?" Ash said.

Her grandmother stood on the roof, frowning.

"Just back off," Ash said. "We'll get—ow!"

A locust slashed at her face, deep enough that its blade grated against her cheekbone. Red blood gushed over her rebreather and she had to tear it from her face or suffocate.

When she looked up, Adaline was gone.

Black dust choked Ash. Her wound pulsed with agonizing fire. "Adaline!" she shouted. Into her comm, she said, "I'm cut. Bugs got me."

"Take the pills," said Juliette.

"What pills?"

Simon came on the line. "Juliette went over all this on our way here. You have a set of pills in your medpack that will fight the poison."

Ash's left eye ached. It was already almost swollen shut. She fished through her pack until she found the pills, vaguely recalling Juliette's instructions. "All of them?"

"No—"

Ash swallowed all five pills. "It'll be fine." Another cloud of locusts swarmed close, but she blocked them from her exposed face with her arm. Her heart thundered in her chest. She blinked through a blurry haze. "Come on, Hector," she said. "Take care of the locust problem, would you?"

More insects swarmed her, pelting hard around the

face and arms. She stumbled to one side, disoriented. Her blood rushed in her ears. Pain subsided, replaced by an acute wave of jittery energy as the drugs kicked in.

"He won't save you in time," said Adaline, stepping onto the roof from a hidden door. She still held the blue glowing dagger in one hand, waving it loosely from side to side in a hypnotic rhythm. "It takes time to integrate. You'll be dead by the time he fully wakes. He will never know what happened to you."

Palak swore over the comm.

"What is it?" Ash panted into the comm. Her mouth was dry and disjointed thoughts raced through her skull.

"Seth's up to something."

Ash looked up to the pyramid towering above them. With a thunderous clap—a hammer on an anvil—the vents opened one notch. Wind rushed through the city as the pyramid inhaled.

Adaline crossed half the distance of the roof, knife raised cautiously before her. "It broke my heart, Ash, when your mother decided to leave this colony. Her betrayal hurt more than you could possibly know"

Fists clenched at Ash's sides, no matter how hard she tried to relax. All of her muscles shook with tension.

"We should have gone up together so that we could return with the new steward. Your mother woke early. She tricked Traverse into accepting her aboard the ship."

"So you followed her."

Adaline said, "When I saw you, I knew she would never return. Traverse would never allow it."

"You traded her for your safety," Ash said through gritted teeth.

"She was to send the steward down when he was ready."

A swarm of locusts covered the roof, wave after wave crawling over Ash and Adaline. Ash covered her face as best she could, but more cuts bit into her exposed flesh. She made her way blindly toward the side of the roof.

As fast as they came, the locusts cleared. The dust-hazed morning sky stretched out above them.

Ash said, "Traverse still lingers here, doesn't it? It's still trying to kill you."

"People like us deserve so much more than Traverse grants. It holds us back, stifling our genius and crushing creativity."

Ash said, "But Victor wouldn't stop."

"He saw that it was possible. The problem hadn't been solved, but the pieces were all on the table. Victor pieced them together and doomed us all."

The locust swarm choked the sky, swinging around to close in on them again.

Ash thought of Seth, and his betrayal of Harish. Her mind still raced from the meds, and she couldn't hold her slippery thoughts still. He was the representative from Victor's castle. "Victor offered Seth immortality."

Adaline opened her mouth to speak, but the locusts hit. They closed in around her, biting and slashing.

Hector.

"Thanks, babe!" Ash yelled.

Adaline charged from the swarm. Her knife flashed and Ash's shoulder burned, but Ash took the brunt of Adaline's momentum in her chest.

They both tumbled off the roof and out of the swarm. The stone street rushed up to meet them, and the clouds of locusts swarmed above. Rays of the green sunrise stretched along this street, parallel to the east-west passage through the center of town. Tentacles waved through the eerie light like waves of golden grass drifting in a gentle breeze.

Gravity had its way, as gravity often does.

There was no pain, only the sudden and oppressive inability to breathe. Ash opened her mouth—to breathe, to speak, to vomit—but nothing came. She held her hand in front of her face and noted the odd angle her elbow took inside her bloodied white suit. Her muscles weren't working right. Her left arm wouldn't move.

Adaline rolled away to stare up at the sky above. She no longer had the knife. Where was the knife? Ash lay on her back as well and soon her lungs started taking gasping sips of air.

Simon's voice came over the comm. "Ash, where did you go?"

Ash choked out the answer. "Queen's gambit."

"That's not how this game works," he replied. He droned on about sacrificing the queen's pawn in an opening move, but Ash lost him in a haze of her own pain.

"Maybe it was a Slav defense," Ash muttered.

Palak swore. "He has the gun." Her voice was laced with pain.

"Why is it nobody can hold onto that stupid weapon?" Ash asked.

Palak snapped, "It's not a very good weapon, and he jumped me. I barely got away. This place is a maze."

Adaline, almost within reach of Ash, started to laugh a low, sad laugh.

"What's so funny?" Ash asked. She pushed herself up and leaned against a stone wall. Sunlight washed over them both. Wind rushed through the city streets.

Her grandmother's head flopped her direction. Bright red blood stained her lips. "I knew this would happen."

"Seth is headed for Hector," Palak said. "He wants the scarab, doesn't he?"

"I should have known," Adaline said. "The heretic couldn't stay away even after all these years."

Ash forced herself into a sitting position. Her left arm still refused to work properly, but she felt no pain. Simon and Palak chattered on the comm, but Ash mashed the button and shut them out. "Victor?"

"He was a prodigy in his day. A mechanist, neuroscientist, and biologist all in one. He knew so much, and we always taught him that there were no limits." Adaline blinked, and her hard gaze focused on Ash. "There are always limits, my dear. There must be."

"He said he could never return."

Adaline drew several long, rasping breaths before responding. "He's sent someone in his place."

"Seth."

"I thought it was you," Adaline choked. "For a moment, I thought it was you."

Another swarm of locusts passed overhead, but none ventured down into the darkening alley.

Adaline grinned, showing bloodied teeth. "Victor was my closest friend. How could I let him destroy himself? What he wanted to make was going to be too much. We tried to banish Traverse, tried to make the machine forget about us. It wasn't enough. Victor had to leave and never return. We had to go into stasis and allow the world to grow. I thought he would die out there, but he still lives. After so long."

Ash saw it now. The knife's blue edge shone under the black folds of Adaline's clothing. It had buried itself nearly to the hilt in her grandmother's side. Blood shone black in the green morning light.

"You're too late," Adaline said between increasingly shallow gasps. "The steward's insertion is complete. He cannot disengage until the city wakes."

"He came here to save your people."

Adaline's broad smile set off a series of bloody coughs. "He will," she rasped. "It will take him a thousand years to bring about our paradise, but he will save them all."

Ash crawled over to her grandmother and cradled her head. "I always wanted to meet you, again."

Adaline's skin grew pale. She coughed more blood. Above, the hammer struck again, and the wind vents opened wider in the pyramid.

Ash reached under her grandmother and pulled the knife from its wound. Blue fire flared, consuming the blood to cauterize the wound. It was too little, too late, Ash knew, but with the knife removed, Adaline gained a little more time. Ash stood. "You're wrong, Adaline Pascal."

"About what?"

"I'm not too late to save Hector." Ash touched a button on her comm. "Juliette?"

"Yes?"

"Are you in yet?"

"Sure am!"

"Then I'm ready."

Behind her, the giant spider rose above the buildings. Its sharp feet scratched stone as it crawled over the rooftops to lower itself into the narrow alley. The front cockpit door opened to reveal Juliette, grinning in the pilot seat. "Finally."

A locust landed on Adaline. Then another. Hundreds descended upon her, and Ash's first instinct was to shoo them away—but there were so many. More and more piled on, cutting. Consuming.

When they flew away, Adaline Pascal was gone.

CHAPTER FOURTEEN

"Do these things really work?" Ash shouted *way* too loud for the small cockpit. She wrestled Juliette's medpack open and found more of the little white pills. Fire burned in her veins.

"You look terrifying." Juliette jammed the controls and launched the spider up over the rooftops.

"What's in these things?" Ash popped another pill.

"Painkillers, speed, something to fight inflammation."

"Will it kill me?"

"How many have you had?"

"Nine?"

"Probably." Juliette furrowed her brow. "Wait, I only gave you five."

"Seven, then?" Ash said, closing Juliette's

medpack and hiding it away. "For sure it was an odd number."

The spider landed hard on the steep slope of the pyramid and clawed upward.

Ash touched her comm. "Simon, how's your plan going?"

"Not great. Harish destroyed the—"

"You're good then? Perfect. There!" The intake vent on the side of the pyramid started to close. "Hurry!"

Juliette yanked the spider sideways and it skittered toward the hole. The front two legs hitched along a violet ridge of stone and sidled up next to the intake.

Before Ash could jump out, Juliette reached over and stopped her. "Hold on," she said. "There's something I need to do."

She took hold of Ash's shoulder and wrist, twisted them into position, and yanked. Ash felt the sickening thump of her elbow popping back into joint. Oh yeah. She had forgotten about that.

"Should that have hurt?" Ash shouted, wiggling her fingers.

"Oh, it will," Juliette said. "It will."

With that, Ash stepped from the spider into the gap. She flicked a button on her grandmother's knife and blue flame crawled up along the razor-sharp edge. Light and heat washed out from it in waves, illuminating the long passage into the center of the pyramid.

"Simon," Ash said into her comm. "Juliette's on her way to you."

As the vent closed with the final hammer strike, the spider dropped from the ledge and leaped high into the air. Ash turned to the tunnel and walked.

"Hector," Ash called out quietly as she walked. She remembered these passages from her time connected to the machine. Her memory wasn't perfect, but she knew she needed to go inward and upward. There were few barriers, but the passages were a confusing maze. "I don't know if you can hear me, babe, but I'm going to go ahead and talk anyway."

Hector, as was his tendency, responded with an oppressive and eternal silence.

When Ash couldn't stand it anymore, she continued, "My grandmother said you'd willingly stay connected to the machine. She said you couldn't abandon the people of this colony, but that's not true. You can. They were fine before we came here, and they'll continue to be fine." It was a lie. If they shut down the main fusion generator, then the situation in the stasis chambers would decline rapidly.

"I need you, Hector. That's what I'm trying to say. However much these people need you, I need you more. And I'm sorry I can't take care of you the way you take care of me. It's not that I think you were designed for it or anything. It's just who I am as a person. I'm selfish, self-centered, and entirely blind to the pessimism that seems to drive everyone else's caution.

"That's why I have you, I think. We're a perfect balance. When I'm being stupid, you stop me. When you're being too cautious, I nudge you into a crazy adventure like this where you get trapped in a machine and indentured into eternal servitude.

"It's not a perfect system, okay!" Ash forced herself to take several long breaths. Her heart rate was a steady drumroll, announcing every danger around every corner and deep in every flickering shadow. The blue light of her knife didn't shine more than a few feet down the black hallways, and a gun-wielding Seth could be anywhere. "Help me out, though, Hector. You don't owe these people anything. Shut down the locust swarms, open all the gates, and maybe turn some lights on. That's all I ask."

Far down one hall, a blue-white light flickered to life.

"Thanks." She pushed a button and snuffed out the light from her knife.

She followed the light down the passage, then, when another light lit the way, up through a narrow gap to a place that smelled of dry dust and burning incense. The light led her to climb a wall to a vent, then through that vent where a mass of wires connected it through a hidden panel to the central chamber. She stopped before opening the panel when she heard movement on the other side. Her hologram had stood in the center of this room, with Hector near the very spot she now hid.

"Is that Seth?" she whispered. She wondered where Palak was in the maze.

Hector answered with silence.

As quietly as she could, Ash opened the panel and slipped into the chamber. Twenty feet away, Seth worked at a console, and in front of him, the doorway to the rest of the pyramid stood wide open. The gun leaned against the console. Its power core hummed.

Ash moved into the room, careful to step lightly with her heavy boots. If she could get the gun before Seth knew she was there, she might get him to back down without a fight.

As she stepped from hiding, she got a good look at Hector. The big man hung suspended in a glass sarcophagus; golden cords attached to nodules in his skull. Attached to the outside of that was a matte black module, now open. Embedded in the core of that was a green beetle, with six legs embedded in the surrounding tech. The scarab. Its lines snaked through the sarcophagus and sunk into Hector's flesh. His expression was slack. Calm. Her heart yearned for him, sought only to embrace him and comfort him.

Hector twitched, and Ash drew a quick breath in surprise.

Seth spun and snatched up his weapon. He leveled it at Ash and a crooked smile crossed his lips. "Thought you'd sneak up, did you?"

"It occurred to me." Her hands twitched.

His eyes flicked to the knife. "Drop the weapon, Ash."

A knife versus a gun. Ash knew how this fight played out. She let the knife fall. It clattered a few inches in front of her foot, inert.

"Now kick it over here."

Ash held his gaze for several long seconds before giving the knife a hard kick. It skittered all the way past Seth to slam against the stone around the doorway.

"Good enough," Seth said, smiling. "You know, Victor said not to tell anyone else about this little side project, but I bet he'd understand the exception."

"He promised you immortality," Ash said. "And he kept it a secret from me because he knew how I'd feel about it."

"And how is that?"

Ash chewed her lower lip—an odd sensation since she felt no pain but still tasted the blood. All her muscles twitched. "I would want to share it with everyone."

Seth shook his head slowly. "You would, wouldn't you? See, it doesn't work that way. Only a few of us get it. The best of us. That way, we're gods to all the regulars out there, and it doesn't disrupt Victor's vision for the future. They live and die in normal cycles. We keep going."

"Is that what Victor promised you?" Ash shot a glance at Hector. He twitched again, and her heart ached for him. "Just godhood?"

Seth gestured at the machine attached to Hector's sarcophagus. "With this, he can give us what we want." His hands tensed on his gun. "Or, he can give *me* what *I* want. What's your choice, Ash?"

Ash took a step to the side, slowly strolling toward Hector. "It's a matter of strategy," she said, scratching her chin. "In the short term, everything in me says I should try to jump you. There's a chance your fancy weapon will misfire or you'll miss."

"Not likely."

"I heard that thing is actually a pretty crappy weapon, and you're probably not going to shoot with this right behind me." She touched the black device connected to Hector. "If you take this to Victor he'll make you immortal at the cost of this entire colony."

"Price I'm willing to pay."

"But not a price he's willing to pay, otherwise, he'd come here himself."

A cruel sneer flashed across Seth's face. "He can make more. Once he gets this one, he can take care of these people."

"I doubt he'd bother." She took another few steps. "Which leaves me with the choice of attacking you or walking away. You have me in check, but what wins the game is checkmate."

"We're not playing games."

Ash ran her fingers through her hair. The pills made her fingers twitch, and her numb fingertips ached under her fingernails. A shadow moved behind Seth, but she forced herself not to look. "You know," Ash said, "there's one lesson I learned really, really well from all my times playing chess with Simon."

"What's that?"

"There's one piece that's way more badass than any of the other pieces. She's fast. Comes at you from way across the board. She's persistent. Unstoppable." She looked at Seth through hooded eyes and allowed a hint of a smile to cross her lips. "The queen."

Palak plunged blue flame into Seth's back.

Seth fired. Screamed.

Ash dove to the side, heat from his final shot burned the air. Seth's bloody, bubbling scream echoed against stone walls, but Palak didn't stop. She yanked the flaming knife from his back, gripped his hair in her other hand, and stabbed him in the neck. The gun clattered to the floor, followed by the heap of Seth's body.

Ash's heart hammered against her ribcage. He'd missed. Ash hadn't known that he would miss. It had been a sacrificial move, giving up herself in the opening moves of a fight so that Palak could win.

"Oh, that's how a gambit is supposed to work," she muttered. She looked to Palak, whose wild dark form stood over the bleeding mess of Seth's body.

But Palak wasn't looking at the body. She stared at something behind Ash.

Ash turned and saw the machine attached to Hector's sarcophagus. A smoking mess smoldered where the scarab had been. It bubbled, burned, and belched, gushing black ichor onto the marble floor like arterial blood from a wound.

Hector's lifeblood.

She rushed to him and pressed her hands against the glass. Her tears mixed with blood on her cheeks and smeared across the glass enclosure.

"I'm fine," he said at length. Only, the voice didn't come from him. It came from the walls around them.

Ash looked up at his face. A single tear ran down one cheek.

When he spoke, his face did not move. "I have to help them," he said.

"You have to help *me*."

"You don't need my help, Ash."

Pulling back, she said, "We have to get you out of this." A klaxon alarm rang, piercing through the pyramid's contemplative silence. She clawed at the golden unit behind his sarcophagus. "There has to be a way to disable it."

"Ash."

The air smelled of sickly sweet of burned flesh. Ash gently touched the tubes running into Hector's chamber. They ran empty, so she pulled them free. Smoking, ruined ends had detached from the device. "Damn," she said. They looked important.

"Ash, stop."

"I can't stop! Hector, I don't care about those people. You're dying." Another alarm sounded, and flames burst from the ruined edges of the machine. She pressed a hand against the glass. "Hector, you have to listen to me. You can't save them. Nobody can save them."

"You're wrong," Hector said. "I can do this." His face twitched, and the gold threads embedded in it flashed a shining light.

Ash stomped out the fire, careful not to do more damage to the machine. The console connection was destroyed, so she had no interface to the systems. "Simon," she said into her comm. "Simon, where are you? I need that tablet."

Silence.

Hector's eyes closed.

Ash was terrible at taking care of her sick boyfriend because he was going to die, and there was nothing she could do to stop it. She dropped to her knees.

Palak backed up against the wall and slid down into a seated position. The blue knife clattered beside her. She glanced down at the blood on her hands, then stared straight ahead.

"Ash," said Hector. "It's fine. I'm fine."

She punched his glass. "You always say that. How can you always be fine? You're hooked up to a machine that's slowly killing you and you're telling me you're fine? This is *not* fine, Hector!" Breaths came in big gulps. "Wake everyone and disconnect."

"There are more than fifty thousand people in stasis here, Ash. If I wake them all at once, they'll starve."

"'Then wake a few and the rest can figure out how to fix their machines.'"

A long time passed, and the smoldering equipment cooled. Ash poked around at the pieces and decided that everything that was destroyed served as life support. Hector's life support. It still seemed somewhat important.

"I am the last steward," Hector finally said, "and I cannot return to this machine once I leave."

"She wanted you for a thousand years. You won't last a day."

"I'll be fine."

The comm crackled to life. Simon said, "We're in position. Should we kill power?"

Ash froze. Killing power might work. She shot a glance at Palak, but the woman still stared uselessly into nothing. If they killed the fusion plant all the way instead of scaling it down, Hector's machine would lose power. He might live.

Nobody else would. Stasis units needed power to engage in the waking sequence.

Ash couldn't breathe. How could she make a decision like this? How could Hector force her to make this decision?

"It's not your decision, Ash," Hector said.

That jerk! She had to make the call soon. It was impossible to know how long Simon would be in position to power down the fusion generators. Her mind raced from the drugs, but it raced through a muddied haze. She couldn't hold one thought long enough to wrangle it to the ground.

"Ash," said Simon. "I need to know. Should I shut this whole city down?"

She looked into Hector's eyes. Without the machine maintaining him, his eyes had gone dry and his face pale. Even in this short time, he looked noticeably worse.

But she could do this.

"Destroy the bad junction, Simon. Harish knows which one. You need to shut down Traverse."

"What?"

"They never evicted Traverse from their network. They shunted their instance into that power junction, and it's been trying to kill them ever since."

The comm crackled. Simon said, "Why wouldn't they just destroy it?"

"Because they thought they could tame Traverse. They made it continue to send supplies from the ship and it assisted them with the development of new tech. That's why Victor can't replicate his scarab technology. For a while, it worked, but Traverse turned on them when Victor went too far." She paced, unable to stand still. "Destroy that junction and Traverse will no longer override the fusion core." Pieces started fitting into place in her head. Maybe this would work. To Hector, she said, "Start waking people, babe. Take as long as you need to do it safely but be as quick as you can."

"That was my original plan," Hector said.

"Then it's a good thing I made that decision." In the comm, she said, "Juliette, I need you to bring your med support system and the food printers into the central chamber."

"Food printers? Why?"

Ash pressed a hand against the glass. "I'm going to keep Hector alive until he can finish the job. We need supplies for several weeks."

"It could take months," Hector said.

"How about weeks?" Ash wasn't sure that her racing heart rate was a result of the drugs.

"Possibly years."

She put her fists on her hips and gave Hector a hard look. "We're going to have a chat about the values of risk-taking and efficiency."

Hector stayed silent.

"And you're not going anywhere, mister," Ash said, "so you're going to listen."

CHAPTER FIFTEEN

ASH TENDED to Hector's needs, and she was pretty good at it. Juliette's med support system kept him alive, providing nutrients intravenously and a moisture film for his skin. After a while, as the rest of the team ventured on the long journey back to Edge, she devised methods of maintaining Hector's muscle mass and preserving organs that kept wanting to shut down. It was nothing like Adaline's scarab, which would have kept him alive and functioning for a thousand years.

There was a key to tending him, she learned. All she had to do was allow herself to care. She loved him as much as she loved herself, even though it meant feeling every pain that plagued his bones and every ache that vibrated in his joints.

It helped distract her from her own pains. She'd have a scar on her cheek and Juliette was right about the elbow. It hurt a lot.

Soon, others woke. Hector revived a dozen at first: agricultural experts who could rebuild Pyramid's living soil using biomass brought back in the bellies of the locusts. They grew plants as fast as they could, producing organic material that would be ready to harvest within weeks.

At which point, Hector would revive more of them. And more.

When, finally, Palak returned, she found Ash elbow-deep in the tubes of Hector's complex life support system.

"Harish and I found almost everything you wanted," Palak said by way of greeting.

Ash ran to Palak and crushed her in a massive hug.

"Aw, yuck, you're covered in goo," Palak said. She didn't try to extract herself.

"Human contact," Ash said. "It's been eternity."

"It's been five days."

"I'm still human," said Hector, his voice still emanating from the walls.

Ash stepped back from Palak. "You don't count, Hector. You're a disembodied voice."

The lights flickered, and a hologram of Hector appeared next to them. His voice still came from the walls. "Am I?"

"That doesn't count," Ash said.

"Whatever." There was amusement in Hector's voice.

Palak cast a glance at the central console, where she had killed Seth.

"You did what you needed to do," Ash said, noticing the look.

"I'm not so sure," Palak strolled to the spot and touched the console as if it might all be an illusion. "Could you have done it?"

Ash very much doubted it. The vision of the knife going through Seth still gave her nightmares. "I could have."

Palak didn't look convinced.

"Talk to Hector about it," Ash said. "He ate my grandmother."

"I didn't!"

"Whatever. The locusts you controlled ate her."

"I marked her as a threat. I didn't know they would do that."

"It seems like a lot of us new arrivals from the ship are capable of things like this," said Palak. "More and more are being sent to live with Victor these days."

"And you?"

"They gave me a choice. I choose to spend time shuttling supplies to your little camp here."

"How is the old vampire anyway?"

Palak picked at a callous on her finger. "Simon got him to admit to everything. Turns out his scarab is failing. He sent Seth to get his research, or, failing that, the second scarab. Turns out he hasn't been able to reproduce the science. Sounds like he's not even sure if he wants to live forever anymore."

"Poor guy."

Palak flicked a speck of dust off the console. "Poor guy almost got Harish killed. Nearly got all of us killed."

Ash placed a hand on the woman's shoulder in a gesture that she very much hoped was comforting. "Exactly what do you mean by *almost* everything."

"We have the soil samples from Victor so the Pyramidians can supplement their microorganisms with his advancements. Harish is bringing your lab equipment and"—she consulted a tablet with a list on it, quoting it—"the biggest screen you all can possibly fit in the back of that stupid spider."

Hector's hologram flickered. "My spider isn't stupid."

"We can watch shows together now." Ash pointed to a place in front of Hector. "Set the screen up here, and we'll be able to—"

"My eyes don't work," Hector said. "You know that, right? I see through the pyramid's systems. You don't need to set it in front of me."

Ash gave him a look. *The* look. After a heavy silence, she said, "We can run the cable along here, and upload shows to the Pyramid network. It'll be like having twenty-first century sitcoms injected directly into your brain."

Palak snorted. "This is your plan to make him hurry?"

"I'm already hurrying," Hector said. "This is her plan to torture me so that I'm grateful once I can leave this thing."

"They're good shows!" Ash cried.

A man in black robes stepped into the darkened frame of the door. He bore a striking resemblance to Orson, but his unkempt hair and deep blue eyes told of a far less orderly mind. Ash wasn't sure if he was a clone or a relative or something else entirely.

"Hey, Kavian," said Ash. "Have you met my friend Palak?"

Kavian pressed his palms together and gave a slight bow. "Welcome." His eyes lingered on the contours of Palak's face. To Ash, he said, "I wish only to tell you that before your steward initiates another waking, we would like to make some requests about who to wake."

"Sounds reasonable," Ash said.

"We would also once again request that you let us help care for him."

"Not a chance," Ash said, trying to keep the weariness from her voice. "I have it under control."

Once Kavian left, Palak said, "Why won't you let them help you?"

Ash looked to Hector's hologram, then to his body. She had cut away most of the glass so that she could better integrate the med support system's hardware. He had wasted away some, but only a little. His muscle mass would diminish the longer he took, but he was healthy. She had, for the most part, succeeded.

"They know best what they need from him," she said. "They're probably great at keeping him alive and functioning for an indefinite amount of time. That's not what *he* needs." She crossed the room and touched Hector's big hand. It didn't respond under her grip, but it didn't need to. "We're closer than we've ever been, and when he's done waking them up, we're going to be able to walk out of here."

"Is it true it's going to take a year?" Harish asked as he carted Ash's biolab supplies into the central chamber.

"It'll take as long as it takes," Ash said, confirming with a nod from Hector. "It'll be shorter if we can convince more of them to move to Edge."

"Shouldn't be hard. They expected a paradise when they woke."

Harish gave her a sideways grin. "Then you probably don't need help setting any of this up."

"I'll have time. Just lean it against the wall."

The big man did as he was told.

"Harish," Ash said, swallowing the lump in her throat. "I wanted to say—"

"Don't worry about it," he said, the mole on his lip dancing in an almost-smile.

"I left you behind."

"To save my sister."

Ash chewed her lip. "Well, I mean, I was mostly

just thinking about Hector to the exclusion of every-thing else."

"Good," said Harish, gesturing at Hector's inert form in the open sarcophagus. "That will give you some practice for what you're doing here."

Once Harish and Palak had brought everything in, they bid her farewell.

"We'll come visit again soon," Palak said. "And next time we'll have time to stay awhile."

"Traverse is back online back home," Harish said. "Recovery is happening, but they really need us back as soon as possible."

As they were leaving, Ash asked again, "What was it you weren't able to bring?"

Palak paused without turning around. After an excruciatingly long pause, she said, "Your media files. Moira wouldn't let us bring any of your shows or books."

"What!"

Palak and Harish wisely left before Ash chased them down. What would she do without media?

She spent days setting up the screens and the lab. The tech wasn't directly compatible with Pyramid's systems, but she managed to make it work. Pyramid, it turned out, had its own media from Earth. There were shows she had never heard of.

But there was more. On her giant screen, Ash ran down through the logs of Pyramid's years of stasis. She expected about fifty years, but it kept going. The records didn't stop after a hundred. Or two hundred.

As far as she knew, the generation ship Traverse had left Earth three hundred years ago.

Pyramid had records a thousand years old.

"There was no oxygen at all when our people first arrived," said Kavian when she asked. "This was a barren rock with little atmosphere and rich deposits of ice."

She sat in the seat in front of her massive screen. "I thought we had gotten to the bottom of Traverse's lies," she said. "I'm pretty sure it nudged me to discover Pyramid. I thought maybe its history held a few more secrets and the occasional genocide, but this..." She gestured at the thousand years of logs. "This upends everything we knew of our journey from Earth. I can't believe the ship arrived here over a thousand years ago."

Kavian pressed his fingertips together. His people tended to use pauses excessively in conversation and it bothered Ash every single time.

Finally, he said, "Pyramid was not the first settlement. Not by many years."

With that, Kavian left Ash to contemplate the fundamental shift in her own understanding of their world. In the end, she came to the conclusion that it didn't matter. What mattered was keeping Hector safe and alive, waking the population of Pyramid in the safest, quickest way possible, and consuming as much Pyramid-exclusive media as possible before the time came to travel back to Edge.

And for that, she was well prepared.

AUTHOR'S NOTE

As always, a special thanks goes out to my wife Carol and my boys Isaac and Gabe. Without their support none of this ever gets to happen.

Huge thanks also go out to my Beta Readers. The turnaround for this one was quite quick, and I could only do it with some stellar input from others. Writing a book may seem like a solo activity sometimes, but I'd never be here if not for support from the Rochester Writers Group, SFWA, and my fellow writers and supporters over on my Patreon. The ability to surround myself with like minds keeps me sane and keeps the words flowing.

Thanks also go out to Scott Alexander Jones for fantastic editing that always seems to find ways to improve and amplify everything I write.

-Anthony W. Eichenlaub